LOVE IN CYBERIA

RED FOX DEFINITIONS

CHLOË RAYBAN

LOVE. IN CYBERIA

RED FOX DEFINITIONS

A Red Fox Book
Published by Random House Children's Books
20 Vauxhall Bridge Road, London SW1V 2SA

A division of The Random House Group Limited
London Melbourne Sydney Auckland
Johannesburg and agencies throughout the world

First published in Great Britain by The Bodley Head 2001

This edition published by Red Fox 2001

1 3 5 7 9 10 8 6 4 2

Printed and bound in Great Britain by Clays Ltd, St Ives PLC

The Random House Group Limited Reg. No. 954009

www.randomhouse.co.uk

ISBN 0 09 941366 3

The Random House Group Limited supports The Forest Stewardship
Council (FSC®), the leading international forest certification organisation.
Our books carrying the FSC label are printed on FSC® certified paper.
FSC is the only forest certification scheme endorsed by the leading
environmental organisations, including Greenpeace. Our
paper procurement policy can be found at
www.randomhouse.co.uk/environment

AKNOWLEDGEMENT

With grateful thanks to Martin Payne

— On-line Marketing Consultant —

for his help and advice on the Internet.

I

I'd been seeing it a lot recently. Hidden among the balloon shapes of the graffiti, tucked in between words like PUNKS and WANDERERS, F.U. and PRUNES, accompanied by Peace signs and Swastikas – cropping up where fly-posters had been ripped off by park officials and alongside the standard willy-and-balls of the totally unimaginative graffiti-ist. Sometimes it was almost obliterated by black and white off-the-peg stencils – sometimes it stood there starkly, all on its own. A single word, written in four plain upright capitals:

LOVE.

with a big full stop after it.

Each time I saw it, I felt with a jolt, that this word was addressed exclusively to me.

I'd seen it on the way home from school that Monday. On a wall that I'd never seen graffiti on before. As if the unknown graffiti artist had left it there, knowing that I would be passing by . . .

LOVE.

I stood staring back at it for a moment. Four stark black

letters on a plain white wall. I considered all over again the questions that went through my mind each time I saw it. Who had written it? Why had they written it? And how the hell did they know that someone as gorgeous as me was going to be reading it? Then I shrugged, threw my school bag over my shoulder and headed for home.

That was the day before the day I grew up. No seriously. I'd always thought that growing up was a gradual process that kind of creeps up on you. That you can't actually tell it's happening – like watching the hands on a clock to see if they move. But that's rubbish. I can actually pinpoint the moment I grew up. I was on top of a number 22 bus heading west down the King's Road.

I was just sitting gazing through the murky window when I saw these tacky bunches of flowers propped up against the Fire Station.

'What are all those flowers doing there?' I asked the bus inspector, who just happened to be scrutinizing the smudge over the date on my now invalid under-16 bus pass.

He peered through the grime and said: 'Oh that. That's for Tom Peterson. Died the other day, he did.'

'But he can't have.' I craned out of the window searching along the pavement. Tom was nowhere to be seen.

The inspector shrugged and continued making his way along the upper deck of the bus.

Tom couldn't have died. I'd checked on him only last Saturday and he'd been fine. He'd even been awake.

Perhaps I ought to explain. Tom Peterson was my own personal good cause. I'd normally see him twice a day from the bus. Once on the way to school and then again on my way back home. Tom was my one little bit of reassurance that there was a life outside school and work – reality beyond that whole treadmill thing that we're all caught up in – commonly known as day-to-day life. I'd be in the bus with all these tied-to-the-treadmill people. They'd all be heads down, destined for offices and interviews, dentists and exams and God knows what. And there would be Tom, waving and grinning, set nicely aside from it all. Tom had lived in the sheltered bit under the Fire Station for as long as I could remember. He was comparatively well off by tramp standards, fully kitted out with a jumbo-sized supermarket trolley stacked with army blankets and newspapers and Sainsbury bags bulging with all those peculiar tramp possessions that don't bear too much investigation.

My visit to Tom had been a ritual I'd secretly and religiously observed every Saturday – when I wasn't hauled away to grandparents or on holiday or something. I don't want to sound as if I want credit for this or anything, but part of the ritual was that each Saturday, I'd give Tom a share of my pocket money. Giving hard earned money away like that isn't as easy as it sounds. You have no idea the agonies of soul-searching I went through when Daddy gave me a raise and I had to work out what would be a fair percentage to hand over to Tom.

I'm not absolutely sure if Tom actually noticed my donations or recognised me or anything. Sometimes he'd kind of wave his dreadlocks or raise a bottle at me, but mostly he'd just continue contentedly muttering to himself. But it wasn't gratitude I was after. No, those small ritual contributions were my kind of insurance. If I missed a week, I'd feel really ghastly, as if something terrible was almost bound to happen. These donations were a defence against the great threatening walls of indifference that I could feel towering around me. I don't want to get heavy here, but you know all the stuff I mean – like Bosnian refugees and wars in Rwanda and holes in the ozone layer and your cat getting run over. Handing over to Tom his Saturday money was my way of fighting back against the awful powerlessness I felt against the weight of all of the bad things that might be about to happen. Somehow, if I could see Tom was all right, I felt the world was all right, rotating round and round just as it should do, with me on it – not about to fly off because gravity had suddenly failed, or freeze to death because the sun had forgotten to rise or anything.

Anyway, all this came to an end that afternoon on the number 22 bus. As the last glimpse of the dusty bunches of wilting flowers slipped from my view, I had to accept the fact that Tom was dead. And all those Saturdays of dedicated financial investment on my part had to be seen for what they were – totally ineffectual against the harsh realities of life.

I hadn't felt so disillusioned since I discovered that the Tag Heuer Daddy brought me back from Singapore was a fake.

So it was an older, thoughtful, more mature, in fact, a 'grown up' me that the 22 bus carried over the transition where the King's Road became, in a quite eerily symbolic way – the *New* King's Road.

Once back at 122 Cheyne Walk, otherwise known as 'home', I hurried up to my room to check in the mirror as to whether my new adult status had actually registered itself physically in the way I looked.

I tried to judge myself objectively. The mirror reflected back: blonde streaked hair, shaggy at the ends where Franz had hacked off the bit we'd over-Sun-Inned – and beneath it, a face the pure unsullied oval of a grade A egg. I sucked my cheeks in so that mature hollows appeared, and scrutinized my collar-bones for the beginnings of salt-cellars. I tried a Kate Moss slump-and-glower.

'You feeling all right?' My mother had thrust open the door and was leaning in looking concerned.

'I do wish you'd knock.'

She swept up a pile of underwear and a couple of coffee mugs from the floor and backed out saying: 'Honestly, Justine. I am your mother.'

'That's what I mean.'

Was there no such thing as privacy in this world? It was going to take some in-depth re-education to make her realise *I wasn't a child any more.*

I cast a glance around my room. Fred Bear stood propped up on my pillow proclaiming the fact that she'd made my bed for me. She'd tidied my dressing table too and put all the caps back on my make-up. I thrust open the wardrobe. She'd even hung my jeans on a hanger. And she'd . . . no she couldn't have . . . yes she had . . . Geesus!

'MU-UM!'

'Don't shout from a distance, darling. And please don't call me by that awful name. Come on down.'

'*What have you done to my jeans*?'

She tried to look innocent.

'I thought they could do with a wash . . .'

'And?'

'Well, the legs were practically hanging off.'

Two absolutely unspeakable Peter Jones iron-on *new* denim patches defaced the backside of my new perfectly-faded, ripped original US 501's.

'You just don't understand anything, do you?'

'I thought you'd be pleased.'

'Pleased!'

'Those jeans were positively indecent.'

'Everyone wears them like that.'

'Well, if you want to go around with your underwear in full view of the world . . .'

'I always wear a "body" underneath.'

'They're nothing more than rags . . .'

'They cost a bomb.'

'And I was coming to that . . .'

'Mummy . . .'

'Quite frankly, Justine . . .'

With those words, I recognised the opening notes of a classic parental tirade. I switched off while it raged. I'll just mention a few trigger phrases to give you the gist of it. 'In my day' . . . 'Saving our pocket money for something worthwhile' . . . 'Not slouching in front of the television' . . . 'When did you last read a book?' . . . 'Taking an interest in current affairs' . . . 'And all those frightful violent films' . . . 'Tennis or swimming or . . . or . . . well outdoor anyway' . . .

Meanwhile, I had put on the kettle, made toast, found a clean plate and knife in the dishwasher and spread two slices of toast with Nutella.

She was in full throttle now. 'And tidy up around the house occasionally and not leave your stuff lying everywhere' . . . 'Or do some of your own ironing' . . . 'Not taking everyone and everything for granted' . . . 'And . . .'

'Do you want tea, Mummy?' I asked as she ran out of steam.

'No, quite frankly Justine, I think I could do with a G&T.'

Sad case, I thought as she disappeared upstairs. I bit into the toast, hot Nutella mixed with butter dribbled deliciously out of the corners of my mouth. Actually, I'm not sure if I totally believed all that stuff about her idealised youth. No one could have been that damn perfect, not even Mummy. And in the Sixties too. How did all that 'sex-drugs-and-bad-behaviour' pass her by? Or had it?

The phone rang.

'Hi . . .'

It was Franz. (Francesca to the uninitiated.)

'You sound a bit off, what's up?'

'Having a domestic.'

'Oh yeah? 'Bout what?'

'Mum's inflicted GBH on my most treasured 501's. They're positively mutilated.'

'Chryst man. How?'

'Obscene patches right across the bum. New denim iron-ons. I tried to rip them off and they left these great gungy black marks. I'm going to have to trash them.'

'Jeez! Poor baby,' Franz sympathised. (Franz is my bestest-bestest friend – she understood the true depths of despair such an event would cause.) 'That mother of yours . . . seriously, you're letting her get totally out of hand.'

'And another thing. I just discovered Tom's dead.'

There was a pause.

'Tom who?'

'Tom Peterson.'

'Oh yeah. Who's he?'

'You know, that homeless guy we used to pass on the way to school.'

'The old wino?'

'The one who lived under the Fire Station.'

'So?'

'He's dead and nobody cares.'

'How do you know he's dead?'

'All these bunches of flowers had been left out for him.'

'So, somebody must care.'

'That's not the point.'

'You care.'

'I know but . . .'

'Justine?'

'Mmm?'

'What's all this got to do with anything else?'

'You wouldn't understand.'

'I think maybe I'd better ring back when you're in a saner mood.'

Franz rang off. She didn't understand. She was my best friend and she had no idea what I was going on about.

I turned this thought over in my mind. I mean usually Franz and I saw eye to eye on everything. We could even go shopping separately and then meet up and find we'd bought exactly the same clothes – freaky. But recently there'd been quite a few things we'd disagreed about.

At this point I had some pretty deep thoughts about the essential separateness of the human condition. OK, don't panic, I'm not going to go all intense on you or anything. I'm just trying to give you the flavour of what it is like to grow up, all of a sudden, just like that – without any warning whatsoever.

I then asked myself, what was the point of being an adult if people didn't treat you as one? Take Mummy for instance, I couldn't even go out of the house without her wanting to know precisely where I was going, when I was coming back, if I had my bus pass/library card/fitness club card/thermal underwear on me, whether I was appropriately dressed for encounters with smart friends of hers/bad weather/potential child-molesters/rogue buses, whether I should consider taking an umbrella/rape alarm/chastity belt . . . etc etc etc. Uggghhrrr!

That evening not just my mother, but the whole world seemed callously unaffected by my shift to adult status. Here I was – same house – same parents – same cat – and the same old TV pages revealing that there was still nothing worthwhile on tonight. I mean boy – I might well have changed but *absolutely nothing else had.* Something had to be done to register my new *mature* identity.

With the kind of grim-faced determination that one sees on the face of a climber about to scale Everest, or lone round-the-world yachtswomen heading out from Chichester Harbour, I went to the utility room and took a large roll of black rubbish bags and headed upstairs. I was about to show the world that I was a different person.

As I passed the sitting room I said to my mother, 'I'm going upstairs. I may be quite some time.'

My mother looked up vaguely from her Harper's & Queen. 'Good idea darling. Get it over with before supper. You'll feel much better. I've put yours on a tray, by the way. Daddy and I have some tedious business do to go to.'

She was obviously under the misapprehension that I was about to tackle my homework.

The task took hours. I literally had to try everything on to prove how inappropriate it was. Here I was, a mature female with a cupboard that seemed suddenly-mysteriously-and-inexplicably full of a child's clothing. In a dumping area in the centre of the room tartan mini-kilts met Benetton separates, Lolita Lempicka designerwear clashed with luminous Lycra Pineapple dancewear – all piling up in an ever-growing graveyard of bulging body bags destined for Oxfam. I wasn't satisfied until the wardrobe had been stripped bare. At last, there was just one pristine set of Calvin Klein underwear left in one drawer and an anonymous pair of black jeans and a black polo-necked sweater in another.

Then I attacked the decor, my Madonna calendar, Take That and Blur posters and my collection of street furniture came down off the walls – even my much-prized 'Danger Men at Work' sign. Shelves were swept clean of their shrines of ornaments, tangled webs of necklaces, dusty cling-ons, sequinned scrunchies, coins, sea-shells, the piece of rock with the glittery bit that might or might not be gold, my almost-complete Smurf collection and a straggling village of miniature Olde Englysh plaster houses. Lastly, the ghastly sun and moon motif sheets and curtains which I'd taken hours deliberating over with Mummy, went into the bags.

By two in the morning I sat in the cleansed and purified room and looked with satisfaction at the walls, bare apart from their little tell-tale bits of Blu-tac. With a sigh, I added the newly unpatched 501's regretfully to the last bag and thrust Fred Bear in after them. Then I re-arranged the only decent item in the room – my stereo with its two speakers set on either side. God the room looked bare. Tomorrow, I thought, real life would begin. Perhaps I should begin by painting my room black . . . or purple.

Downstairs a key turned in the lock. I switched the light off. Footsteps could be heard on the stairs below. There was a muffled giggle and my parents' bedroom door clicked shut.

With any luck Mummy would have a frightful hangover tomorrow morning and I'd be able to get out of the house, complete with bags, without being spotted. I curled up under my coverless duvet and then climbed out again, rescued Fred, climbed back into bed with him and fell contentedly to sleep.

The lady in the King's Road Oxfam Shop must have thought it was Christmas. The shop wasn't actually open when I arrived at 8.30 am weighed down like a bag lady, but I hammered on the door until one of those wizened little smiley people that seem to belong in Oxfam shops popped up from behind a vacuum cleaner and opened it for me.

She staggered away beneath the weight of the bags, and then came back and stuck a 'Save the Children' sticker on my lapel and said I was a kind, thoughtful girl. So I went on my way to school feeling like a positive 'saint'. So-oo virtuous! The feeling lasted all through the day right up until I arrived back home.

Mummy didn't actually see things in the same light. Quite honestly, I wonder about her sometimes. She spends the majority of her life 'Staunchly-Supporting-Causes' and 'Doing-her-bit-for-Charity' but when it comes to acts of pure unselfishness like 'Giving-Away-All-Your-Clothes', that charitable spirit seems totally to desert her.

Even when I pointed out that 'I wouldn't be seen dead in any of those old things again anyway', she continued to rant on about extravagance and selfishness and all those clichés adults tend to fall back on when they're rendered helpless by rage.

'You'll just have to go to the shop and ask for them back,' she insisted.

'I can't. It's nearly five, they close at half-past.' I didn't add that it would mean I would miss *Neighbours*.

'Right!' she said. 'That's not a problem. I'll drive you there.'

'But Mummy . . .'

'No buts . . . get in the car.' Her face was turning a threatening shade of puce.

I climbed in beside her and sat glumly staring through the window as she crashed through the gears until we screeched to a halt outside Oxfam.

I don't generally believe in Divine Intervention. But it seemed that maybe that afternoon 'Someone' must have been looking down from above and helping my possessions along on their way to providing a pump or a bag of seed-corn, or a couple of hundred hoes or whatever, somewhere far away in some sun-baked land with a name made mainly of consonants.

'Caroline! What a surprise! It is Caroline Morton isn't it? How are you? And is this, no it can't be. Is this your daughter?'

The wizened little smiley lady had been replaced by a large-boned woman who was wearing a smart linen suit. She was kissing Mummy on both cheeks.

'Muriel. Well I never. What are you doing here?'

A long dialogue ensued about farmhouses in Shropshire and problems at Lloyds with a bit about rough shooting in Scotland thrown in for good measure.

I wasn't really attending. I was casting a wary eye over the rows of hangers and spotting, here and there, familiar garments now accessorized with little Oxfam price labels. My Pineapple dancewear was even stretched in an uncomfortable knicker-up-the-crack way over the dummy in the window.

A girl about my age with a ring through one nostril came out from behind a curtained-off area that acted as a changing-room, dressed in a pair of my Pucci stretch luminous leggings. She was wearing them with a sequinned cocktail top and an angora cardigan. They looked fantastic.

'I'll have them,' she said to Muriel.

'That'll be three pounds. Do you need a bag?'

'No sweat. I'll wear them.'

Mummy and I glowered at each other.

'So . . .' said Muriel to Mummy. 'What brings you in here?'

Mummy's eyes rested on a large poster from which a group of wide-eyed and very hungry-looking people stared back at her.

There was a pause.

I held my breath while a rare expression of moral conflict passed across Mummy's face.

'Place mats!' she said, grasping a raffia set decorated with wonky brown storks. 'Such fun. Give the guests a talking point.'

'And for such a good cause,' agreed Muriel.

Five minutes later we were back in the car with the raffia mats in a crushed Tesco bag.

'OK, so why didn't you simply ask her to give us my stuff back?' I asked.

'I just couldn't bring myself,' said Mummy. 'It would have been just too, too humiliating.'

It seems that Muriel had been Head Girl at Mummy's old boarding school. The sight of Muriel must have resurrected something of her flagging fair-play and the 'honour of the dorm' mentality. Or as Mummy put it in a quite weird reversion to dated schoolgirl slang: 'Once one had handed over one's togs, a chap couldn't simply go and demand them back.'

2

Have you noticed all those ads in the media for things with names like Cybacrom and Tecnoc? They promise to revolutionise your life and give you instant access to all those things you never knew you couldn't get at. They look innocent enough, but in actual fact they're part of a great undergound movement that is trying to take us all over.

They're 'spearheaded' by these guys who go around trying to look really anonymous wearing grey business suits and hi-tec trainers. Daddy was holed up with one of these in his study for hours on Saturday. He called himself an 'Infotec Advisor' and arrived with a huge briefcase bulging with glossy brochures. I had been to tennis coaching, been coached, showered, changed, and was coming back by the time he left. They shook hands on the front step and Daddy said:

'Well, I dare say you know best. No point in stinting and spoiling the whole show, eh?'

And the guy passed me with an expression on his face like a cat that's just finished licking double Jersey cream off its whiskers.

Three days later this van arrived with 'COMPU-MINE' written on the side and a group of men dressed in white coats carried in all these huge cardboard boxes with enormous care as if they were filled with high explosive.

They disappeared into Daddy's study and I heard snatches of muttered 'dialog' through the door saying things like:

'Input to VDU check positive.'

'Output port positive. Hey they've given us an RS249!'

'249? Never get up to 28800 bps out of that . . .'

When they'd finished setting everything up, I popped in to see what the damage was.

They'd infiltrated. It was staggering! Daddy had been completely taken over. He had everything, colour screen, laser printer, CD-Rom, modem, scanner – you name it. It must have cost a bomb! And to think that he had actually refused to get me a mobile phone. Honestly, the injustice of it all.

When Daddy arrived back that night he stood in the doorway of his study for some moments surveying the set up with a look that I would describe as somewhere between apprehension and panic.

He was very quiet over supper and made for his study straight afterwards and closed the door behind him.

When I popped my head round the door an hour or so later he seemed to have mastered how to turn the monitor on.

'All pretty straightforward so far,' he said.

I nodded.

As I went up to do my homework I could hear keys being hit spasmodically – I left him trying to type a word with two fingers between bouts of low muttering.

Five minutes later he appeared at my bedroom door with a manual in his hand.

'Do you know anyone who would understand this?'

I was looking for an excuse not to start on my History assignment. This assignment was the brainchild of Ms Shaw our history teacher. It was called the 'Millennium Project'. Each of us had been given the choice of a different decade of the twentieth century. Since it seemed the coolest and had the best clothes, I had decided to do an analytical study of the Sixties.

I was doing some dedicated research by reading up the fashion tips in an ancient copy of a magazine called *Honey*. I'd found this magazine under the playroom carpet so I reckon it qualified as a 'prime source'. Ms Shaw, made a big fuss about prime sources. She used to say things about 'History being all around us' and that it was all still there 'In the very molecules of existence' – as if you were going to find particles of Gandhi ash in the fluff of your blazer pocket or something – which is theoretically possible really if you come to think about it.

Anyway, Daddy's problem seemed to be far more urgent than sorting out The Millennium. At any rate it gave me the perfect excuse to break off.

So I rang Chuck.

Chuck's been a friend of mine forever. At least from practically before I was born. You see, his mother and my mother met at Queen Charlotte's antenatal classes when Chuck and I were round about the same size bulge. And as luck would have it, both my mother and his mother went into labour on the same day. Chuck was born at 4.30 pm and I was born at 5.00, so we're kind of unrelated twins. Of course, he's always trying to pull rank because of his age advantage, but basically we're best mates.

It just so happens that Chuck is a real computer freak. For the first fifteen years of his life no one had seen anything of him but the back of his head as he was bent over a console.

If anyone could sort Daddy out, Chuck could.

'Hey, guess what. The Antiques are trying to update to

the twentieth century. My father's bought all this infotec gear. He's attempting to get into the Net.'

'Do I hear a cry for help?' asked Chuck.

'If you're not terribly busy.'

'It's only the sixth time I've tried to get to grips with this probability equation,' he said.

'Sounds like you could do with a break.'

'Don't let him think I'm sorting out his problems every time.'

'Thanks Chuck.'

By the time Chuck arrived, Daddy had become practically ballistic over the incompetence and simple-mindedness of the people who write the 'bloody manuals'.

'If you can understand this convoluted load of gibberish you're a better man than I am,' said Daddy.

Chuck looked at the manual with contempt.

'First rule,' he said. 'Never use a manual. All the information you need should be in the Memory.'

'Re-ally?'

Chuck proceeded to try and explain to Daddy in plain layman's language how to find his way around. After twenty minutes he moved a notch down from the plain layman stuff and was using words of one syllable and guiding Daddy's nervous finger on the keypad. After a painful half-hour he'd managed to teach him how to find the day's share prices. Chuck wrote out detailed instructions on how to do it on a sheet of paper in the improbable hope that he would be able to find them on his own next time.

Daddy was ecstatic. He headed off to watch the Ten o'clock News content in the knowledge that he was now 'computer literate'.

'Do you mind if I use it to type up my homework?' I asked as he made his escape from the study. I'd come across a couple of articles in *Honey* that I reckoned could be fruitfully recycled if I typed them in.

A broad smile of relief appeared on Daddy's face. Suddenly this wildly expensive computer system had switched from being a lunatic impulse purchase in a moment of weakness to being 'Educational'.

'Feel free,' he said.

And with a gesture of abandon he threw the *Financial Times* into the wastebin.

'Who needs it?' he said.

'Do you think he'll be able to manage on his own now?' I asked.

Chuck shook his head sadly. 'NFWM,' he said.

'What's that meant to mean?'

Chuck explained painstakingly, 'NFWM is a TLA – or "Three Letter Acronym" for the uninitiated like your innocent self meaning "No ****ing Way Man".'

'I make NFWM four letters,' I pointed out.

'Yeah, so OK. So what?' said Chuck.

And in typical male way when defeated by female logic he decided that he'd better get back home to console himself with his equation and left me to it.

I spent the following two hours discovering that 'word-processing' was just a rather grand title for two-finger typing. The apostrophe seemed to be lurking out of sight somewhere up among the exclamation marks and numbers. At any rate, I couldn't locate it, so my version of the *Honey* articles had a certain originality, with strange words like 'Dont' and 'Arent' littering the pages. I finished at around midnight only to find that the system had been supplied and delivered with everything except paper, so I couldn't print out. But, no problem, I could simply transfer what I'd done to a disk and print-out at school. There was a handy little pile of grey ones right beside the computer. I popped one in and tapped what seemed to be the appropriate keys.

Do you ever get those patches when absolutely nothing goes right?

Just when I was congratulating myself on my mastery over technology, the monitor started making ghastly static noises – the kind of VDU equivalent of electronic last gasps. And then would you believe it? *It wiped the lot.*

I could not believe my eyes.

Six whole pages in which I had so painstakingly typed my own highly personalised version of the articles. All I was left with was a blank screen with a warning icon in the shape of a little black 'bomb' ticking away in a menacing fashion in one corner. I switched the screen off and went to bed fuming.

Friday was a bad day. Daddy had popped into his study first thing to check the Dow Jones share index and switched on to find the evil little 'bomb icon' featuring prominently on an ominous grey screen. He stormed into my room roaring totally out of line things about getting a 'hacker' in to put it right and subtracting the cost from my pocket money. I spent the whole day in a generalised kind of fury against all things technological, computers in particular.

Next morning – which was a Saturday – things hadn't improved much. Mummy had come upstairs to wake me three times. And on the third time totally lost her cool. You know, I never have understood this peculiar adult inconsistency about sleep. They are perfectly happy for you to slide into bed hours and hours early at night time and waste countless precious evenings sleeping. But for some unaccountable reason, come the morning, the same activity becomes a *crime*. I was having a really worthwhile dream that morning, too. She kept waking me up just as I was getting to the good bit. Just as I was about to give Brad Pitt the snog of his life, our lips were, so poignantly, *just-about-to-touch* . . . Now I may never know what snogging him is like. And I reckon Brad Pitt must've felt pretty let down too.

Frankly, she'd ruined my morning. I lay in bed not feeling Saturday-ish at all. I stayed there trying to identify the precise cause. Apart from Brad Pitt not having his life made meaningful by me, there was something else. It was some moments before I realised what the problem was. It was a kind of empty void where Tom used to be. And since Tom wasn't there any more, the main reason for my Saturday morning trip up the King's Road had ceased to exist.

I stared at the ceiling and tried to think of something worthwhile to do instead. And failed. So I got up and went downstairs to make a cup of tea. That's when things started to go from bad to worse. There were two letters for me on the mat and I thought: Great. Cool man. Someone cares.

Inside was note from Henry (Henrietta) accompanying a letter from her mother demanding, in a very uncalled for way, that I should refund her the £60 for the black dress of Henry's I'd borrowed and which I had left casually hanging over my bedside lamp, and which being of a very poor man-made fibre had caught fire. She claims it seems to have mysteriously 'shrunk'. Maybe she had latched on to the way I kind of 'incorporated' the burnt bit into the side seam? I considered counter-claiming Henry had put on weight. Bad scene man.

The other envelope was from NatWest. Frankly, these banks are very very short-sighted. I mean here am I – real star quality, likely to make an absolute fortune in the very near future and they're fussing over a measly £97.32 overdraft.

Finally, the hall mirror added the unwelcome information

that I had the very tiniest, I mean *really minuscule* blemish on my nose. Three misguided seconds later I had turned it into a landmark. I'm telling you, all I could see in the mirror was one great massive spot with a person attached to it.

So I made a mug of weak sweet tea as treatment for shock and sat down with it trying to recover some vestige of interest in life.

Daddy had left the *Saturday Times* on the kitchen table. I sat sipping my tea and scanning the headlines. An item in the lower right hand corner of the page caught my eye.

> TRIBUTE TO KING'S ROAD CHARACTER
>
> Mourners gathered at the graveside this week of vagrant Tom Peterson. The funeral, paid for by an unknown benefactor, took place yesterday morning at Putney Cemetery. Numerous floral tributes bore witness to Tom's popularity as a Chelsea character. Further bunches of flowers piled up outside Chelsea Fire Station – one of Tom's favourite haunts.

Suddenly, I knew what I had to do that day.

The woman in 'Fab Flowers' tried to sell me a wreath. But the way I saw it, it was bad enough being dead, one didn't have to rub it in. So I chose this massive bunch of really cheery flowers – orange marigolds, cerise asters, a load of scarlet gladdies and some really bright yellow lilies, and I asked for a big red bow on it too. I figured Tom would have liked that.

Then I set out for Putney Cemetery.

Since this was a pilgrimage it didn't seem right to take the Tube. I wasn't going to crawl there on my hands and knees exactly, but I could walk. So I trekked south to the river and took the footbridge that leads over the Thames to Putney.

They're heavily into graffiti around the Putney Bridge area. There's one wall that's got more layers on it than a plate of Alphabetti Spaghetti. And in the midst of the multi-coloured tangle of bloated letters I saw something that brought me to a halt. There it was again . . .

Four black characters standing out of the jumble in a totally eerie way as if left there just for me.

LOVE.

It looked freshly painted. Almost as if the mysterious graffiti artist had known that I would be going this way, on this day, across this bridge that hardly anyone knew about, and very few people used. Weird man.

I continued feeling the intensely significant weirdness of it all as I crossed the bridge. Beneath, the river was sliding by, sludge green, oily and silent. Above, the clouds were skudding past, steel grey fingers, evil and windswept. And I was on the bridge like some transcendental tightrope walker, strung between the two. (That's just a small sample of how weird I was feeling).

The other end of the bridge, in that nether-world they call South London, I came down to earth. I mean, you can't continue feeling weird in Putney for long. Putney is so ordinary they ought to put a plaque up to commemorate it. It's got Boots and M&S and Sainsbury's and loads of gift and card shops where Putney people go to buy things like scented floral drawer liners and mug trees and personalised fridge magnets to give to each other. Beyond the High Street are miles and miles of anonymous streets serviced by video shops and take-away restaurants, so that all these Putney residents can stay inside their identical Putney houses and not venture out unless there's a war or something. As I made my way along the silent streets, I could visualise them behind their net curtains, keeping up the good work, boring for Britain.

Anyway, to guide me through this netherworld, I had my trusty A-Z London Street Atlas. Reading the A-Z is always a tricky manouvre when you're heading south – all the roads you're trying to get down, most inconveniently, seem to be the wrong way up and all the right turns transposed into lefts and vice-versa. Eventually, I resorted to holding the book upside down and at last I found my way into a street that called itself, most promisingly: 'All Souls Lane'. Sure enough, at the end of it there was a sign which said: 'To the cemetery'.

The cemetery had an impressive grey brick castellated gateway – it towered over me in a most uninviting gothic sort of way. I walked through wondering if this was such a good idea after all. There were miles and miles of tombstones all looking very sombre and self-important – proclaiming the fact that they had every right to be there. I felt very much too young and too alive and totally out of place.

I was just at the point of deciding that this whole trip was a total mistake and was about to turn on my heel and leave – in spite of the fact that I had invested an absolute bomb in the bunch of flowers – when an official-looking sort of chap came out of a building marked 'Lodge' and said, 'Can I help you miss?'

'I'm not sure. I mean, I'm looking for someone's grave – Tom Peterson's?'

'Recently interred?' he enquired in official graveyard language.

I nodded. 'This week.'

He consulted a list. 'There you go. Last Thursday. You'll find him right over on the far side.'

He pointed me in the right direction and stood watching as I made my way up the main avenue towards the distant prospect of the railway line. I was tempted to turn back a couple of times but every time I looked round, I found he was standing there watching and waving me on.

I ventured on beneath the disapproving gaze of stone angels, between the grand family mausoleums built like miniature palaces and past the cosy double tombs of loving couples with their bright marble chippings and plastic flowers. There were thousands of them, old stones tipping and toppling, belonging to people with old-fashioned names like Albert and Maud and inscribed with grand words that I was sure that none of the people underneath would ever have used in real life. I continued through newer ones, their lettering freshly carved and some of them seemingly still tended.

At last, I came to a windswept area that had earth and bootmarks trodden into the path. There were a lot of fresh flowers and in the centre I spotted a simple white cross with the words Tom Peterson ? – 1997.

I stood there staring at it, feeling rather foolish. I wondered if I ought to say a prayer or something, but I'm not really religious and I'm pretty certain Tom wasn't either. A tube train passed at that moment and I was glad for Tom that there was a nice jolly-sounding every-day noise going past where he was buried, breaking through the silence of the cemetery in a cheery sort of way.

I was just bending over adding my flowers to Tom's pile when I heard a voice.

Honestly, I'm telling you man, I nearly passed out from shock.

I swung round and this guy was standing just a few yards away from me. He was really oddly dressed in a long black mac almost to the ground. It was undone showing a black sweatshirt and black jeans. He was dressed all in black apart, that is, from a pair of silver moon boots.

'Sorry if I freaked you out?' he said. He paused and looked thoughtfully at the flowers. 'Cool flowers. Tom would like them.'

I nodded, speechlessly.

OK, so let's admit it. This wasn't just shock. I mean I hope this doesn't sound tasteless or anything in the context, but under all that black gear I'm telling you, this guy was so-oo fit. I mean, he was gor-geous. Tall, nice build, tousled hair that kind of looked as if it had been tie-dyed, hint of stubble and the most hypnotic blue eyes ever seen on this earth. He was the kind of guy you always dream you'll meet and never do. And the oddest thing of all was finding him here – in a graveyard of all places – freaky.

'I kind of thought he'd prefer something bright like this. They'd cheer him up. I mean, if he were alive that is.'

The guy didn't seem to be phased by this totally naff speech of mine. He just nodded and said: 'Sure thing. You a mate of his?'

'Yes . . . no . . . not really,' I said. 'I used to see him every day when I was on the bus, on my way to . . . And then on Saturdays, I always go up up the King's Road and . . .' God, I wasn't going to admit that I was still at school or . . . Cringe! that I used to give him hand-outs. 'I mean, no I didn't really know him at all,' I finished lamely.

'Tom was a free spirit . . .'

I nodded.

'Up until this happened.'

'True . . .'

'Ironic isn't it. A bloke can spend his whole life fighting for the right to have no fixed abode – in and out of court or clink, rounded up and hassled, never getting any peace. Then someone goes and well and truly knobbles him. Pins him down like, for eternity. Seals him in and then shoves a great official tombstone bang on top of him. The poor sod.'

I hadn't thought of it like that. But I nodded in agreement.

'Had to come and see it for myself.'

'Sure. That's kind of why I came,' I said

A chill wind had started up and I felt a spot or two of rain. I struggled with the zip of my jacket.

The boy leaned over and settled my flowers more firmly in the centre of the grave then he stood back glowering at them.

I hovered, feeling awkward.

Then, quite suddenly, he swung round to face me.

'It's raining,' he said.

'Yes. I know.'

'Guess we ought to be going.'

'Yes.'

I got this kind of thrill from the way he said, 'we' like that.

We walked back towards the gate in silence. The graveyard looked really bleak and mournful in the rain. Suddenly it made the idea of cremation seem quite a jolly sort of alternative. All bright and warm by comparison.

'Would have been better to cremate him, I guess.'

'Or upload him,' he muttered.

'Upload?'

'Yeah. Upload.'

'What's that meant to mean?'

Our eyes met. It was like sinking into deep pools of icy water. Geesus this guy was so-oo gorgeous.

'You wouldn't be interested,' he said and kicked a stone along the path and then bent down, picked up another one and threw it as far and as hard as he could.

We soon reached the gates of the cemetery and I could tell he was going to head off and with my kind of luck I'd never set eyes on him again. There was a café on the other side of the street. And the rain was coming down hard.

'I could kill for a hot chocolate,' I said.

Five minutes later we were seated at a greasy table with chipped cups of hot chocolate. I was starting to wonder if this qualified as a pick-up. I mean I never normally pick up guys, it's strictly against my principles. I figure if males like the look of you it's up to them to do the up-picking. And if they don't, you're on to a loser anyway. But I hadn't exactly offered to buy him a hot chocolate, he'd just kind of tagged along. And he'd bought us two Kit-Kats, so I guess that made us even.

Anyway we'd soon established the basics, like we each had a name and his was 'Los' which was a pretty unusual kind of name but as things progressed I discovered that Los was a pretty unusual sort of guy. I mean, if he'd said he was an extra-terrestrial who'd just crash-landed in the cemetery and I was the first humanoid he'd come across, frankly, the whole thing would have been more credible.

Anyway, our first halting and totally cringe-making conversation went something like this:

'So what's all this up-whatever it was?'

'Uploading?'

I nodded.

'You wouldn't be interested.'

'I wouldn't have asked if I wasn't.'

'Nah . . . it'd take too long to explain, you wouldn't understand.'

'Try me.'

He took a sip of hot chocolate and leaned over and fiddled with the laces of his moon boots. He gave me a sidelong look.

Boy this guy was so gor-geous. And I don't think I was flattering myself when I say that he actually seemed to think I was pretty cool too. I mean, man, the air was practically electric between us.

Or maybe I was imagining it.

'You know anything about infotec?' he asked looking at me searchingly.

Oh God, he wasn't staring at my nose was he? I mean, I'd done a pretty good job with the Coverstick, but what with all the rain and everything . . .

'Ye-es, a little.' We were on to tricky ground here.

He shrugged.

'A little! As I said. You wouldn't be interested.'

'No I didn't mean that. Really. I think the whole thing is fascinating – riveting . . .' I prompted. Geesus, maybe I sounded as if I was trying too hard!

You know, the trouble with the whole relationship thing is this. Guys who are really and truly staggeringly attractive never actually fancy you. They're always after some girl who is even more staggeringly attractive than they are. On the really rare occasions that an absolutely 'fit' guy takes an interest in you, you start to have doubts as to whether he's so terribly 'fit' after all. So you never get it together. At least, that was the grim story of my love life so far. But this time it was different. I couldn't be imagining it. I could feel that Los really fancied me. And I don't need to spell out how I felt about him.

'So what's so riveting about it?' He was kind of half teasing and half not. Testing me out I guess.

'I've still got quite a bit to learn,' I backtracked. (A nasty little image of the 'bomb' crept into my mind at this point. I ignored it.) 'So go on. Tell me more.'

He shrugged and continued: 'Uploading is the opposite of downloading.'

'I see,' I said, not seeing in the least. So, I added the standard phrase that Daddy had taught me for getting more information without sounding like a total wally: 'So what does uploading entail exactly?'

'Entail?' he said going over the word slowly as if he'd never heard it before. 'Entail *exactly*?'

'I mean,' I stammered. 'What the hell does uploading mean?'

'OK,' he said, tipping his chair back and eyeing me in a calculating way. 'Listen carefully.'

He then launched into a total load of unintelligible techno-babble. He was talking fast but with a dead flat matter-of-fact tone of voice as if nothing he was going to say was likely to get through to me and he couldn't really be bothered to try. 'Uploading is like converting all your data into bits and scanning them into a computer so that you can transfer your existence to dataspace.' He ended, then paused and took another sip of hot chocolate. A delicious rim of foam settled on his upper lip. God he was so-oo yummy.

'Do you follow me?'

'Ummm, yes. Definitely.'

He frowned and continued. 'Once you're uploaded you can simply surf the waves. In dataspace you're just information like everything else. Time and space don't mean a thing. You could spend forever say, surfing the Net.'

The Net! I didn't believe I was hearing this. The Net is just for nerds. Losers like Chuck and all those lonely people who want to spend a lifetime finding out what the weather is like in Rio, or what colour knickers are the current rage worldwide. Wasn't cruising the Net the 90's equivalent of stamp-collecting?

'Isn't that kind of – boring?'

'Sometimes, sometimes not. Depends on the waves,' he shrugged.

'That's surely not what you do all the time,' I continued suspiciously, 'surfing?'

'And other things too. Like music – I do keyboard and vocals, in a group.'

This was reassuring.

'Would I have heard of you?'

'We've just had our first world tour.' He was obviously trying to impress me without being too blindingly obvious. But basically I don't fall for this kind of male posing – I needed concrete evidence – he'd have to do better than that.

'Then I must have heard of you,' I prompted.

'Depends . . .' he said. He was fiddling around with the squeezy tomato-shaped sauce dispenser – squeezing it to make a little bubble of sauce come to the top and then letting it get slurped back again.

'Amazing,' he said.

'What's amazing?'

'Simple pneumatics. No mechanics, no power source, yet it works.'

'That's ketchup for you,' I said in a humouring kind of way. This guy was really a one-off. I mean weird or what?

'Anyway,' I said, getting him back to the point. 'What does it depend on?'

'Whether or not you've got access.'

Somehow I didn't think he was talking about a credit card.

'Access.'

'Yep.'

I wasn't getting far along this tack and I didn't want to sound really stupid. If he was just teasing – playing some sort of joke on me – the way boys love to do, I wasn't going to get taken in too easily. On the other hand, if he was serious, I didn't want to sound too stupid. Either way I couldn't win.

'So what's the group called? Where do you hang out?'

'I'll give you our number. Got anything to write on?'

I located an old envelope and scrabbled round for a pen in my bag.

I couldn't be hearing this. Here was the most drop-dead-gorgeous piece of male machinery I'd ever set eyes on and *he wanted to give me his number!* At last I located a chewed Bic.

He took the envelope and examined it slowly, scratching at the stamp with his thumbnail.

'Snail mail,' he said as if he'd never seen an envelope before. Then I handed him the Bic. He took the little blue plastic bit out of the top and then pushed it back in again.

'The genuine article.' He shook his head and smiled. Weird man.

Then very slowly and painstakingly he wrote on the envelope and handed it back to me.

Our eyes met.

'Thanks,' I said, my knees turning to jelly as I got another dazzling flash of piercing blue.

'So . . . looks like the rain's stopped,' he said.

Then he picked up his mac saying ultra-casually, 'Look us up some time.'

And he dived out of the café without even giving me a backward glance.

'Look us up some time.'

Us? The group probably. Well, at least I'd got his number.

Or had I? There was nothing on the envelope but:

http://www.love@3001ad.com

'Great . . .'

3

When I got back home there was a message on the answerphone from Franz to the effect that her elusive father, who spent most of his time lurking somewhere in Switzerland, had turned up again and that he was paying for her birthday dinner and it was going to be on Saturday.

I got on the phone right away.

'He says eight of us can go to a restaurant and he'll pick up the bill. Cool eh?'

'So who're you inviting?'

Franz gave a quick run through the obvious ones. The list went something like this:

Males:

Alex – generally accepted as the horniest choice on the current male menu – and didn't he know it! But good to be seen around with 'cos if guys think he thinks you're cool your rating goes sky high.

Chuck – not an obvious choice maybe, but he's grown lately so we don't tower over him any more. And since he worked on that organic farm last summer, where they were so into alternative energy they'd kind of used him like a human fork-lift, he'd even got some muscle on him. After the farm thing, Franz had actually taken him in hand for a while and he'd, at last, learned the basics. Like how to prop a female up against a wall when he snogs her so he doesn't overbalance when overcome with passion. And his acne had miraculously cleared up overnight. Funny that.

Jason (Franz's half-brother) – essential because he's into the London Club scene and would get us all into some venue free in which to hang out afterwards, on the downside, means we have to include his girlfriend Lulu who has a little girl voice and thinks she should go into modelling, if she could only get up early enough to get to castings.

Females (there were three of us who had been right through school together and we never did anything without the other two):

Franz (Francesca): our hostess of the night – who basically has the most pulling power of the terrible trio, I mean she doesn't need to wear a Wonder-bra to get noticed, and her legs aren't bad either.

Henry (Henrietta): who we always thought was going to turn out a swot 'cos she's into things like Physics and Chemistry in a big way, but who surprised us all by suddenly growing 34inch legs and Jerry Hall cheekbones overnight and is generally considered quite a Babe.

Me: I wouldn't really like to hazard a guess at rating myself. Seven-ish out of ten, variable with occasional brilliant patches maybe. I guess when I'm all dressed up and made up and ready to go out I'd score around an eight . . .

Or maybe seven's more realistic . . . ? When I'm *dressed up* – I suddenly had an awful thought . . .

'Hang on a minute, I'll ring you back!'

'Mu-um,' I called over the banisters.

She must've gone deaf or something . . .

I tried again.

Eventually, 'Are you calling me?' came from below.

'Yes, actually.'

'Then could you call properly please.'

'What do you mean, *properly*?'

'How many times have I asked you not to use that dreadful word?' Her face appeared below with an affronted expression on it.

'But "Mummy" is *so* childish.'

'And "Mum" is so . . .' she paused.

'So what?'

'So,' she was searching for a politically correct way of describing class-consciousness. (There isn't one).

'Everyone in our family has always called Mummy; Mummy,' Mummy continued as if this put an end to the matter.

'It sounds ridiculous from a person my age.'

'What do you propose to call me then? Caroline? Honestly, I don't know what's got into you lately, Justine . . .'

'Nothing's got *into* me. It's just that times have changed, *Caroline dear*.'

'When I was your age . . .' she started.

I interrupted before she could get into full throttle.

'Look. Please listen. I've got a real problem. Franz is having a birthday dinner on Saturday and I haven't got a thing to wear – I mean literally!'

There was another resigned sigh.

'And whose fault is that?'

Before I could negotiate any concrete financial agreement, the phone rang again. Franz was back on the line. She'd done a quick count and discovered we were still one man short for the dinner. Could I think of anyone?

Could I think of anyone? A vision of hypnotic blue eyes swam before my eyes. Could I think of anything else?

I gave Franz a quick run-down of Los's looks, style and sexual potential.

She was suitably impressed.

'So what does this guy do? Is he still at school or at college, or what?'

Maybe I'd exaggerated the extent of our relationship a wee bit. I didn't like to admit I had no idea, so I said: 'He's in a group. He does vocals and keyboard.'

'Boy! What kind of music are they into?'

This was a tricky one.

'Electronic mainly.' I improvised. 'Ambient Techno with a touch of Jungle, kind of an Indie sound with Britpop overtones.' (I reckoned that should pretty well cover everything.)

'What do they call themselves "Dog's Dinner"?'

I ignored this comment with dignity.

'Their music's pretty radical actually.'

'Sounds like it! OK. Let's invite him. You know where to get hold of him?'

'Sure. No problem,' I said.

I got on to Chuck right away.

'Chuck. Look you've got to help me.'

'If you want me to phone that school of yours again, it's not on. I could tell last time I didn't fool them for one moment . . .'

'Nonsense, you can take off Daddy perfectly . . . But it's not that. I'm desperate. I need to get hold of a man.'

'Look no further. I can be round right away. Massage first? Or just straight sex?'

'Be serious, just for one moment, please.'

'So it's not my body you're after. Curses. Sob. OK. Shoot.'

I explained about the meeting and gave him a slightly

watered-down version suitable for male ears of what I thought of Los's eyes, body, dress sense and general potential. Chuck went very quiet at this point.

'And this "dick-on-legs" left you with his e-mail address?'

I ignored the crude reference and straightened out the envelope. (It had got somewhat crumpled from being stored next to the skin). I read out the address.

'Well I guess you could always have an e-romance,' said Chuck with a most unfeeling snort of hilarity.

'But I want to find him for real,' I pointed out. 'In the flesh.'

'Could be tricky.'

'Oh pl-ease. You could. You're so-oo brilliant at things like that.'

Chuck wasn't falling for flattery so easily. 'You could yourself. Seeing as your dad's spent mega-bucks on all that gear. Why don't you just dial up this nerd yourself?'

'Small problem.' I explained about the bomb.

Chuck let out a low whistle.

'Honestly Justine! How the hell did you do that?'

'How was I to know those grey disks weren't ordinary floppies? Couldn't we do it at your place?'

'My kit's so antique it takes half an hour to scroll up the options menu.' He sounded for a moment as if he was about to slide into a fit of male gloom about his low technological status. Then he cheered up and suggested, 'Tell you what, though. We could meet up in Cyberspace.'

'Cut the techno-babble. Translation please.'

'Cyberspace is a café. Got all the latest stuff. Loads of monitors you rent by the hour. We could meet up tomorrow, have a coffee there and use their gear to have a mosey around the Net – access that e-mail address, all that stuff.'

'Cool. Where is this place?'

* * *

'This place' was, suitably enough, tucked away round the back of all the video and audio shops in Tottenham Court Road. I forced my way up the street through dense crowds of electronically-obsessed bargain hunters.

The café had a flashing neon sign outside saying: CYBER-SPACE in digital letters. By the cigarette smoke wafting out through the open doorway you could tell it was popular.

I hesitated on the threshold. Remember that café scene in *Star Wars*? The one at the end of the Universe that was full of aliens? Well, I'm telling you, man, Cyberspace is the terrestrial equivalant. This is where Anorak meets Kagoul. It was full of them, all heads down, minds bent, each intent on their own glimmering VDU screen.

There was not a sound in the place apart from the soft background patter of fingertips on keypads.

Chuck was nowhere to be seen. Typical! I tip-toed over to the bar feeling totally out of place.

The girl behind the cash till eyed me doubtfully. 'Do you need any help?'

Hey, this was a café after all. Reassuringly, there was a glass dome with an assortment of cakes underneath and packets of various herb teas on a shelf behind her to prove it.

'Could I have a cup of tea?' I asked.

'What kind?'

'What's the choice?'

'Camomile, Rosehip, Mint, Cinnamon and Apple . . .'

'Do you have ordinary tea . . .'

'Do you want time?'

'Thyme?'

'On the Net?'

'Oh that! Yes, definitely.'

'That'll be £3.50 then for half an hour. Is this your first time?'

I was feeling hot and bothered and heads were turning in our direction.

Having to admit you were a 'Net virgin' in company like this was *really* embarrassing.

'No problem. I've used my father's Apple-Mac,' I said with what I hoped passed as confidence.

'OK. I'll get you set up and you can see how you go.'

She seated me on a bar stool in front of a colour monitor that bore no resemblance to the one at home whatsoever. It bore the message:

'Welcome to Cyberspace – Your Gateway to the Net' in electronic colours.

'Just click on anything you want. And call one of us if you want help,' said the girl.

I took a sip of tea for mental strength and clicked on the first box which was marked e-mail.

The screen over-reacted violently and most of what was on it disappeared. I was left facing a blank page with loads of little boxes at the top. I waited for something to happen. Absolutely nothing did.

The boy next to me was typing with such intentness and at such a speed you couldn't even hear the gaps between his fingers hitting the keys.

I looked around for the Cyberwaitress but she'd disappeared. This was ghastly. I hadn't felt like this since I opened my examination paper in GCSE maths. I could positively sense everyone in the room sensing me doing nothing.

Where the hell was Chuck?

All around I could feel glassy screen-focused eyes bearing in on me. I reached for my bag. The precious envelope Los had written his e-mail address on was secreted away in an inner pocket.

It was one of those bags that has a really long shoulder strap. As luck would have it the strap had got hitched round something. So I gave it a really hard tug. That's when the guy next to me kind of flew off his bar stool. It wasn't really my fault. I mean those bags should have a 'Safety Warning' or something.

Anyway, once we'd got him untangled from the bag strap and back on his stool and discovered that he wasn't hurt and I'd bought him a fresh cup of tea and the general uproar had died down a bit, Chuck arrived.

'Am I glad to see you.'

'That's nice. What's been going on. Why's there tea everywhere?'

The Cyberwaitress who was mopping up around us gave a glance in my direction from under a raised eyebrow.

'What kept you!' I hissed.

'The Enterprise. It must've taken off of its own accord. I looked everywhere, then found it under the bed.'

Explanation: Chuck has this Star Trek Alarm Clock. It's his most treasured possession. It's the only alarm clock that's ever managed to get him up in the morning. It's built like a space launcher and covered in flashing lights and stuff. And when the alarm goes off you hear Spock's voice saying: '*The Enterprise is under attack. Get up and DO something!*' And it does it in Klingon too. I think maybe when Chuck bought it, he might have been under the misapprehension that it'd give him pulling power or something. Like 'wake up with me darlin' and it'll be some morning!' Sad case.

'I see you've made your presence felt,' said Chuck when he got a decent view of the blank screen.

'Come on, let's get on with it before we run out of time.'

'OK. Got that address? Tap it in then.'

I typed? 'Http/www/love:@//3001ad.com', in a very professional fashion.

Chuck sighed: 'Come on let me do it. You have to get every single dot and stroke right, to get through.'

I moved over and let him take my stool. God these machines were pedantic!

He tapped in: 'http://www.love@3001ad.com'. Under Chuck's hands the monitor seemed quite miraculously to understand instructions and respond with obedience. It patiently purred and bleeped in a very professional fashion.

We waited what seemed an age. Then, at last, coloured graphics started to appear on the screen. Rough at first and then scrolling up until there were three people staring out of the screen and YES you couldn't miss those hypnotic eyes. The one in the centre was Los.

But it wasn't those eyes that I was staring at. It was the message on his T-shirt. They were all wearing them.

They said: LOVE.

'Look,' I said. 'That's really weird, man. That logo on their T-shirts. I keep seeing it everywhere! LOVE. It's just such a freaky coincidence. Like it was *meant* or something.'

Chuck shrugged. 'It's just a TLA – the first letters of their name. It spells it out underneath, see: "Lords Of Virtual Existence".'

'But it's weird, man. It's just so . . .' I was lost for words.

'Naff?' suggested Chuck.

OK, so we were obviously in for a predictable dose of male competitiveness. I ignored his comment and studied the screen. There were two people with Los. A massive guy in a black leather jerkin on drums and a girl who had puce lips and what looked like midnight blue hair but maybe this was just the poor quality of the electronic colours.

My eyes returned to Los. God he was so-oo horny.

'Listen I've got to find where this guy hangs out. How do I go about it?'

'Well I guess we could click on to e-mail and ask for his home address,' said Chuck. 'That's if you really think it's worth it. He looks a right wally to me.'

'Yes, I do as a matter of fact,' I said.

'Lords Of Virtual Existence,' he snorted. 'Geesus what dweebs.'

'Let's get going or we'll run out of time.' I didn't like the tone Chuck was taking – dweebs indeed.

He started clicking like mad on the mouse and then he typed in:

Need to connect.
Request your current location
Respond to http://www.cndjd@cyberspac.co.uk

'That should do the trick.'

'So what happens next?'

'Depends when they check their 'mail. They might not respond till tomorrow.'

'Great!'

'On the other hand,' he said catching sight of the chocolate cake under the cake display dome. 'They might be looking in right now. So it's worth hanging around till our time runs out.'

I bought him a slice of chocolate cake and a cappuccino and got another cup of tea for myself. Geesus this was costing a fortune. We sat gazing at the blank screen as Chuck ate.

'Good place this,' said Chuck between mouthfuls.

I gazed bleakly at the clientele. By their general posture, I reckoned cyber-hunch-syndrome is going to be *the* epidemic of the next millennium. Most of these certainly seemed to be storing up serious back-trouble for the future.

What a waste of life, I thought.

Then just as we were about to give up, our screen leapt into life and a message came up.

From:http://www.love@3001ad.com
To:http://www.cndjd@cyberspac.co.uk
We are the Lords Of Virtual Existence
Who are you?

Chuck and I exchanged glances.

'Don't think they'll be wildly interested when we tell them we're two jerks sitting in Cyberspace,' said Chuck.

I shrugged. 'Guess you've got a point there. Maybe we should make ourselves sound a bit more interesting.'

'Leave it to me,' said Chuck. And he typed in:

From: C. Newton-Dwight Jnr
of Spielberg Productions Inc
To: The Lords Of Virtual Existence.
Need to confer over potential album deal.
Please supply your location IRL

'That should do the trick,' he said.

'What's IRL?'

'In Real Life,' said Chuck, with a sigh. 'You really don't know anything, do you?'

We didn't have to wait long for the answer.

From: Lords Of Virtual Existence
To: C Newton Dwight Jnr Spielberg Products Inc
Our IRL address is:
67, Pratts Lane, Southfields.

'I can see why they wanted to keep that one to themselves,' said Chuck.

4

It was all very well to have Los's address. The problem was – what to do with this vital piece of information.

There were numerous options. I considered them in no particular order of desirability. I could fill a sports bag with dusters and stuff and ring on his doorbell posing as a door-to-door salesperson. I could get a Saturday job at one of his local shops. I could stand on his street corner selling *The Big Issue.* Or take my sleeping bag and live in a neighbouring doorway. Or maybe I should simply hang around outside his house and pretend I just happened to be passing when he came out.

Somehow none of these alternatives seemed to have quite the charismatic quality of the meeting I'd ideally plan for us.

What I needed to do was to meet him *accidentally* on neutral ground. That's how I happened to find myself on Earl's Court station platform on a wet Saturday morning.

It had taken a long time to firm up on this step. Not least was the problem of what to wear. I'd scoured the King's Road for the right outfit. I'd tried on so many alternatives, shop assistants were starting to recognise me and cower when I came in. I tried the retro-hetro-skinny-mini-thigh-boots look and the Ralph Lauren baggy-shaggy-waistcoat-look. I'd tried hi-tec-sportz-chic, flirty-fluffy-baby-doll, Op-Art-It-girl, and the flowery-hippy-long-and-loopy Monsoon look. I'd tried ethnic, gothic, and synthetic. I'd dragged my body up and through and in and out of mohair, angora, rubber, leather and vinyl. I'd even trailed back to the Oxfam shop and tried on some of the stuff I'd given away. In the end I'd gone home and I'd taken a long hard look at myself in the mirror. I was wearing the one outfit I had left. Calvin Klein underwear, black jeans and black polo neck. Well, I didn't want to look as if I was trying too hard, did I?

I had calculated that for people from Southfields, Earl's Court tube station must represent the gateway to civilisation. Anyone who went anywhere was bound to pass through there sometime.

I started my vigil at around 10.30 am. Nobody normal could possibly be up and around before then. One thing I soon discovered was that standing around doing nothing certainly gives you an appetite. By 11.30 I had visited the station health food kiosk three times and was at risk of OD-ing on fruit and fibre. I had consumed a banana, a packet of nuts and raisins and two wholefood muesli bars. And by mid-day I was so au fait with the trains that passed through that I could distinguish an eastbound from a northbound District Line simply by the way their doors were operated. By 12.30 I was starting to wonder if I ought to risk making a frantic dash to Dunkin Donuts for some real sustenance.

It was at this point that a northbound District pulled in. I couldn't believe it. A figure in a black mac swept past. He was hunched in a carriage near the front, head down, reading. Yes, I was certain now. It could only be Los's tousled tie-dyed hair.

I swiftly moved along the platform to the neighbouring carriage and leapt on to the train. I positioned myself with the professional nonchalance of an experienced Private Eye, slouching against a pole at the front end of the carriage. This way I could keep an eye on his movements.

I stood rocking to the rhythm of the moving train in an agony of anticipation. Only two panes of London Transport dirt-ingrained glass separated us. He continued to sit, headdown, deep in concentration over some magazine he was reading. Nothing happened until we reached Notting Hill Gate station.

Then, he looked up, suddenly realised where he was, leapt to his feet and headed off the train. I narrowly missed being cut in two by the closing tube doors as I hurtled after him.

Hovering behind a conveniently large lady, I followed at a safe distance as he made his way along the platform and up the escalator. He continued through the barrier without looking back and made off towards Portobello Road.

Portobello Road is a long narrow street that has a massive market every Saturday morning. They sell everything. Leather gear and antiques, second-hand clothes, candles and craftware, wooden toys, bric-a-brac and bygones, silverware, jewellery, posters and prints, pot-pourri, massage oil, handknits, cycle masks, naughty knickers and luminous socks. And all these are jumbled up with people, people, people. People of every height, width, colour, age, race and sexual inclination were on the move everywhere. And today, under a steely sky spitting a continuous driving drizzle, they were all conspiring together to obscure my view from the one thing I was trying to keep my eye on – Los.

I tailed him as he wove his way in and out of dripping, flapping, shouting obstacles. He disappeared at times between streams of damp browsers, or tired tourists clumped around dogged street performers. I followed, fighting off tangles of bags and balloons, dogs-on-leads, eye-threatening umbrellas, ankle-grazing prams – narrowly avoiding bell-ringing cyclists and stumbling over knee-high kids. And then, just as we reached the far end of the market where the crowds eased off a bit, I lost him.

This was the grotty end where the stalls got tackier and all sorts of lost looking people stood around. There were piles of rubbish lying on the ground and greasy discarded fish and chip papers blowing in the wind. The second-hand clothes stalls soon gave way to ones selling food. I searched frantically through stalls piled high with strange Caribbean stuff – all kinds of alternative vegetables like yams and red bananas and spiky green fruit shaped like mines and some things so strange and knobbly and hairy they could only be there for curiosity value.

And then I saw him. He was crossing the street. My heart missed a beat as he was momentarily hidden by a load of people weighed down by a battered piano. I wasn't going to let him get away now.

He had, at last, slowed down and he was hesitating outside a bar called 'Seventh Heaven'. Then, all of a sudden, he looked to left and right and dived up a neighbouring stairway and disappeared from sight.

I hovered wondering what to do next.

There was a phone booth which, most conveniently, provided a safe vantage point from which to observe the stairway. It was raining pretty hard by now so I climbed thankfully inside. I stood there for a good ten minutes fighting back against a fug of steam which kept building up on the inside of the glass.

There was a tap on the window. A woman with an unmistakable I-need-to-make-an-urgent-call look on her face, was tapping with her phonecard and glaring at me as if she thought it was about time I came out.

If I was going to maintain this position I was going to have to call someone. I reached in my pocket for my phonecard and called Franz.

Her voice was all breathy with sleep.

'Hi there, man. What you doing calling me at this ungodly hour?'

'I just had to call someone. It's one o'clock anyway.'

'Why're you sounding so cloak-and-dagger?'

I hadn't realised I was whispering.

'I'm in a phone booth in Notting Hill and you'll never guess what. HE's inside the building right in front of me.'

'Who?'

'The guy. The one I want to invite to the party – Los.'

'Oh him . . . (yawn). What's he doing?'

'No idea, he's inside and I'm outside.'

'Doing what?'

'I'm in a phone booth.'

'Not you, him?'

'How should I know?'

'I worry about you sometimes, Justine . . .'

'What do you think I should do?'

'Get inside and ask him if you really want him to come . . . (another yawn).'

'I can't just appear out of the blue!'

'Find some excuse then. What are you waiting for? Geesus, Justine, the party's tonight for godsake. DO something before it's too late, I gotta get some sleep.'

'I can't.'

'I don't believe I'm hearing this. You've bored the knickers off us all week about this guy. This is your big opportunity.'

'What shall I say?'

There was a groan from the other end. 'Are you being a total dweeb or what?'

The woman outside had resorted to a continuous drumming of her phonecard on the window.

'OK. But I'm blaming you if I make a right idiot of myself.'

I replaced the receiver with some force.

I opened the door of the phone booth and took a deep breath.

The woman squeezed past me with a most uncalled-for expression on her face.

There was a large sign on the wall which flanked the staircase which read:

WYSIWYG UNIT 22
PC's / MULTIMEDIA / CD ROM/ PRINTERS
AUDIO VIDEO INTERNET RELAY
New & Used Hardware
All types software
CONVERSIONS
Yo! You name it. Man . . . !

I headed up the stairs. The building was one of those industrial blocks that had once been a factory or warehouse or something and now was divided into units cut off from each other by vast metal concertina doors. I could hear voices coming from beyond one of these doors which was marked Unit 22.

The door was open just a fraction. I peered in. The room was absolutely stacked from floor to ceiling with computer stuff. It didn't look very new and a lot of it seemed to be in the process of being dismembered with wires hanging out and bits of their insides spewed over workbenches. In the centre sitting on a crate was Los. He was talking to a guy who looked like a tramp. He had long grizzled grey hair down to his shoulders. The guy was nodding his head and saying:

'Whatever you want, man . . . I can fix you up.'

The Wysiwyg guy indicated something on his workbench, I strained to hear what they were saying but they had their backs to me craning over the table. I couldn't catch anything else.

I stood there glued to the spot. 'Fix you up'. I mean I'm not suspicious by nature but I'm not stupid either. It was a funny area round here. Several guys had come up to me in the street offering to sell me grass or coke and I don't think it was lawnseed or Coca Cola they had in mind. And all this computer stuff. Not new. All being taken apart. I mean, it didn't look as if it had just been bought from Dixons . . .

Then, quite suddenly, both Los and the tramp guy got to their feet.

'Yo man,' he said and slapped Los on the back. 'Be in touch soon-as. Watch how you go, eh?'

Their meeting was obviously coming to an end. I turned and bolted back down the stairs. I could already hear quick footsteps coming down the concrete steps behind me.

I shot back into the street again. Maybe Los was into something really dodgy? Then I remembered those hypnotic blue eyes. I thought back to the way he'd been in the café, with the ketchup and the biro and everything. OK, so I couldn't make him out. But I couldn't imagine him doing anything bad either. There was something weird about him but it wasn't bad-weird. Or was it? No it wasn't. Trust me, OK? My instincts said Los was a regular guy. And they told me without a shadow of doubt to *go for him, man.*

So how far had I got? Actually, this was getting serious.

So far, I had wasted a whole Saturday morning on this guy and still hadn't reached the epic point of saying 'Hello'. The question was, how was I going to '*move the relationship forward*' without humiliating myself by letting on that I'd followed him?

I thought fast. I figured that if I turned off down a side street and then doubled back, I could just about meet up with him in the street in a suitably accidental manner. At any rate this was my last chance so I really had no other option.

I headed down the nearest side street and took two sharp right turns. Sure enough, as I came round the bend – *we met face to face.*

He did a double take.

'Hey! Chance meeting you, again! Hi there!' he said.

'Hi – what are you doing here?' I asked, hoping I looked surprised enough to see him.

'Just about to ask you that myself.'

'Just passing by.'

'Serendipity!'

'Freaky.'

'Umm.'

There was a 2,000 volt pause.

'How goes?' he asked.

'Fine.'

'It's raining again.' He put out a hand indicating rain.

'Umm.'

(Sorry about this. I know it was a pretty uninspiring conversation.)

'Well, I guess I better be on my way,' he said.

Here goes my opportunity, I thought.

'Which way is that?' I asked.

'Which way are you going?'

I indicated back in the general direction of Notting Hill Gate.

'Me too,' he said which was kind of odd considering he'd been walking in the opposite direction. But then, who am I to talk?

'So what are *you* doing here?' I asked.

'Had to fix something up,' he said, seemingly without a trace of guilt. 'What brings you here?'

I cast around for inspiration,

'Oh, just getting a few things from the market.'

'Uh . . . huh.'

Just to reinforce the point I paused at a stall selling an assortment of ill-shaped warty looking objects.

'What can I do you for, dearie?' the stallholder held out the scoop from his scales, expectantly.

'Err . . . some of that?'

'Root ginger? How much do you want, luv?'

I wasn't awfully sure how you bought root ginger.

'Couple of kilos should do it.'

'Some like it hot,' said the stallholder with a raised eyebrow. 'That'll be four quid. Go easy on it now.'

'Sure will,' I said and exchanged the money for a knobbly pink plastic carrier bag. Great!

We walked on up Portobello Road. At least Los walked. I glided about two inches off the pavement. If I hadn't been weighed down by the plastic carrier I think I might well have floated off altogether.

Halfway up the market we met this guy. Hang on, I'd seen him somewhere before. Yes, it was the drummer from the group.

As they met, he and Los exchanged a weird kind of handshake. It was somewhere between a high-five and something out of Star Trek – a linking of fingers and an upward and outward movement. Los put an arm around my shoulders and pulled me forward in a matter-of-fact sort of way as if we'd known each other for ages and introduced the guy as 'Phil'.

'Phil. A Delphia,' Phil added and linked his fingers in mine in a lowish 'five'.

'Come an' bev, man,' he said. 'And bring er . . .'

'Justine,' I said.

So I found myself in this bar full of the wildest looking people. Los wove his way through the crowd and made for a table on the far side of the room where a girl was sitting. She looked up. Her hair *was* midnight blue. It was the girl from the group.

'Hi,' she said when she saw Phil. And she gave Los a lazy kind of look from under her long fringey lashes.

Have you ever felt yourself bristle from envy? I'm telling you man, I could feel the little hairs on my back literally stand on end. These two must have something going between them.

She introduced herself as: 'TeXas with a big X'. Geesus I felt lame having a totally ordinary name like Justine. Actually, I felt pretty lame altogether. Los's friends were much older than mine and looked as if they were independent of home and education and all the paraphernalia of day to day life that basically drags one down.

And between themselves, they spoke a different language too. I mean it was English all right but the words were combined in a way that I'd certainly never come across before. I'll give you a sample.

Phil: 'So what's with the retro-chick taking up your ether, man.'

Los: 'She's OK. Glossy. Friend of an NFA, recently de-animated.'

Los got up and went over to the bar.

'You two currently connecting?' asked Phil jerking his head towards Los.

I assumed he meant 'going-out-together'. (*I wish!*) I shook my head. 'We only just met.'

'How? . . . Where? . . . Tell?'

'In Putney Cemetery as a matter of fact.'

'Uh huh,' he said as if this were the most normal kind of meeting place in the world.

Los came back with three glasses full of dark steaming liquid with green bits floating in it.

I looked at it doubtfully. 'What is it?'

'Mint tea with honey,' he said. 'Try it. No caffeine, no alcohol, nothing that's going to blow your brain cells.'

Which was handy, actually, because my brain cells were forced into overdrive over the next half hour or so.

I sat there listening to them nodding like a noddy-dog and feeling as if I'd become part of life's wallpaper.

TeXas, with the big X, didn't say much. But she looked so-oo cool. She was dressed in black velvet apart from laced to the knee boots which were silver like Los's.

She didn't seem to have any problem following the conversation, so I couldn't fall back on the lame excuse that all this talk was boy-stuff and not part of my world. I mean these people were so heavily into infotec they made Chuck seem practically normal.

Los was going on about the deal he'd managed to do with the Wysiwyg guy in the warehouse.

'He's setting up a broadband – CDL for us to use prime time twelve hundred GMT.'

'Yeah? What's that in Big Apple?'

'Minus six.'

'How's he slicing the connect time?'

'He's downloading a w32s125.exe – that should give us 2287298.'

'And for OLE support? Where do we locate that?'

Los reached in his pocket and brought out a crumpled scrap of paper. They all leaned over it. From where I was sitting it read something like this:

http://www.voyagerco.com/cdlink/getstarted/win.html

'It's self-executable,' continued Los. 'So we can use it to shift all we want in the DL directory.'

'Cryonic,' said Phil.

I had taken refuge behind my mint tea and was sipping with rapt concentration.

Actually, I was starting to wonder whether it was such a wildly good idea to invite Los to the party tonight. I mean, could I really imagine this guy sitting down and eating a meal with Henry and Franz and Co. I mean culture clash!

And worse, Los coming to pick me up from home – because Mummy would probably insist – and having to sit on Mummy's best striped brocade sofa and get cross-examined with all Mummy's photos looking on. The ones of me and my sister Jemima as Brownies, me smiling like a cabbage patch doll 'cos I'd no front teeth.

And worse still! Having to bear the embarrassment of all the showing off – all those silver framed pictures of Daddy's yacht at Cowes and his half of the racehorse he owns with those blokes at the office . . .

When I looked up both Phil and Los were staring at me.

'You cross lining with me?' said Phil.

'Uh huh, Venus?' said Los.

'Virtual,' said Phil. 'Will she, though?'

'Do what?' I asked, I could feel myself going red under so much delicious male scrutiny.

'Be Venus for us?' said Los.

'On-line videolink?' said Phil.

'In a video? I asked.

'Kind of,' they nodded.

'Why pick me?'

'Your face is the girl's in the lyrics.'

'Really?'

'Yep, precisely, how I visualise Venus.'

'What would I have to do?' I asked. I could just imagine what my mother would say to me being in a video with some absolute strangers I'd met in a bar.

'Just your face which we'll edit in over a starscape.'

It sounded pretty straightforward, clothes-on kind of stuff.

'When?'

'Tonight.'

'Tonight?'

Tonight was Franz's party. But so what? A sixteen-year-old birthday party was kid's stuff. They'd all behave in a totally juvenile fashion and it would probably end in a food fight anyway.

So I said, 'Sure. No problem.'

Frankly, I'd do anything for Los. Everything about him was a million miles away from anything or anyone I'd ever known before . . .

'Onward and outward,' said Phil raising his glass.

'Onward and outward,' I said.

'To Cyberians wherever they may surf,' said Los.

'Siberians?' I asked. This could explain some of their unusual behaviour.

'C. Y. B. E. R. I. A. N. S.' Los spelled the word out.

'Who are they?' I asked.

'Cyberpunks, time's troubadours, fugitives from the big bad tomorrow,' said Phil.

'Oh I see, sure,' I said. 'Er . . . Cheers!'

Boy, I was totally out of my depth.

While the guys were busy tying up some loose ends about what to do with all Wysiwyg's 'Voyager-via-cdlnkins-exe' stuff, TeXas leaned forward and said, 'Mind if I give you a bit of advice?'

'No sure. Feel free. Go ahead.'

'Don't try to upgrade the relationship.'

'What relationship?'

'With Los. Seen it happen so many times.' She gave me a knowing look.

'I don't know what you're talking about. We only just met.'

'These surfers. They're obsessive . . . Unreliable . . . Here one day, gone the next. Take my advice.'

'I think I can judge for myself thank you,' I said coolly. Who the hell did she think she was? He-llo, I get it now. It was so-oo obvious. She wanted Los all to herself. Well, who could blame her?

'He's only hanging round now because of the album deal,' she continued.

'Album deal?'

'With Spielberg. They said they'd get in touch *real* soon.'

'So have they been – in touch?' I asked innocently.

'Not yet. But he reckons it's worth hanging around on the off-chance.'

I nodded and agreed and smiled back in a knowing sort of way.

The conversation got heavily into 'cyber-culture' after that. I tried to give a good imitation of 'intelligent interest'. By the time I left the bar I was kind of staggering from pure mental exhaustion.

I made my way home wondering if I'd made a total wally

of myself. I mean, they'd talked about things that had never even grazed my consciousness. I kept going over what I might have said or done. I must have seemed like a total air-head. Maybe I was really stupid. I mean if I were, I'd be the last to notice, wouldn't I?

The result of all this painful introspection was that on the way back to Notting Hill Gate Tube, I *invested* the money Caroline had given me to buy something 'smart and suitable' for Franz's party, plus the money she had given me to pay back Henry for the dress I trashed, in a long black down-to-the-ankle number and a can of silver spray paint.

5

It just so happened that, as luck would have it, Chuck came round that afternoon to take a peek at Daddy's computer and see if he could put it right before a 'hacker' had a chance to rip us off.

I sat and looked on while Chuck did arty things with 'Apple' and 'esc' and a combination of other random and seldom-visited keys. He muttered consoling and encouraging noises to the computer as he did so.

Suddenly the bomb disappeared, the screen flashed three times in a melodramatic way and then leapt back into life. Chuck leaned back in his chair with a proud-but-modest expression on his face waiting for praise.

'So . . . what exactly was the problem?' he said.

'OK. I admit it. You're a star. How do you do it?' I said.

'Natural born genius,' he said. 'Either you've got it or you haven't.'

'Is there anything you don't know about computers?'

'Not worth knowing.'

While Chuck was in helpful-mode, it seemed a good time to pump him on anything he might happen to know about my *new friends*.

'Have you ever heard of people who call themselves Cyberians?'

'Inhabitants of the former U.S.S.R.? Heavily into furry hats?'

'C. Y. B. E. R. I. A. N. S.,' I spelt it out for him.

'Oh cyberpunks – in the Net?' (Now I was talking his language.) 'Maybe. There are stacks of weird cults on the Net.'

'This isn't a weird cult. It's a load of people with some pretty radical scientific views actually.'

'Like what?'

I paused, I had to get this right: 'Like uploading your consciousness into a computer so that you can cruise dataspace and travel through time.'

Chuck snorted with contempt and then he chuckled. I knew he was hooked. This was just the kind of stuff that Chuck really got a kick out of.

'Typical cyberpunk junk. How come you're so interested? Doesn't sound like your sort of thing to me, Justine.'

'Let's just say I met these people.'

'What people, where, when?'

'This morning. In Portobello Road. I'd met one of them before . . .'

'Not that dipstick you picked up in the cemetery?'

'He's not a dipstick, he's a really interesting person actually.'

Chuck had obviously been getting a lot more low-down on Los from Franz. Honestly, males just can't resist gossip, can they?

He was leaning back in the chair and watching me with an assessing gaze. I could feel myself getting hot and bothered under his scrutiny. He let out a low whistle. 'What a female will do when she's gets the hots for a bloke.'

'Rubbish,' I said. 'That's got nothing to do with it.'

'Is it his soul, or his *body* you're after?'

'Both.'

'What, that jerk in silver moon boots?'

'Oh belt up. You're just jealous, that's all.'

'Jealous! That's rich! Me jealous of such a nerd – poseur – dweeb – geek – brain-challenged neanderthal . . .'

He was running out of insults.

'Anything else?'

'The bloke is off the wall, man! Either he's a phoney or barking mad.'

'He is not . . .'

'OK. I'll prove it. Let's look these "Cyberians" up,' said Chuck, turning back with determination to face the screen.

He started typing in the word 'Cyberia'.

After a lot of dweeping and gnittering noises, the screen flashed into life and started scrolling up with a mass of unfathomable looking information.

'Here's their "Homepage",' said Chuck.

'Oh, this is glorious,' he added with a whoop of laughter. 'Just listen to this!'

What's a Cyberian? See FAQ list of answers. Check the list of FCP's – Famous Cyberian Persons. Phil A Delphia: X1 Essay: My Life in Dataspace. Cyberian interests include transhumanism, robotics, cryonics, artificial intelligence, personality uploading, neuroscience, nanotechnology, techno-musicology

'What a load of bollocks,' said Chuck.

I dismissed this as pure male envy.

'That's because you don't understand it,' I said defensively.

'Who says?' said Chuck.

'Explain it then.'

'OK. I will.'

Chuck rapidly read down the screen mumbling to himself and then he made me sit down in front of him and pay attention.

The gist of what he said went something like this.

'OK, so basically they're a load of brain-challenged phonies who think they're geniuses because they're into all these off-the-wall "alternative" theories . . .'

'Like what?'

'Like cryonics for instance . . .'

'What's that?'

'Basically, it means, when you reckon you're going to croak, you pay a load of money to some jerks who tuck you up all cosy in a deep freeze. They keep you there for a couple of millennia, or until someone comes up with a cure for death or something. Then they pop you in a microwave set on de-frost and you leap back into a full and active life. Personally, it's not my idea of self-preservation, but may be yours.'

'Cool!'

'Very.'

'And then there's nanotechnology.'

'Nanotechnology?'

This was all about borrowing theories from biology and applying them to other things – but since my biology studies ended with the dissection of the worm, I was a bit out of my depth on this one . . .

'Then there's memetics,' he continued, 'which is all to

do with replicating agents . . . and bionomics and . . . (had enough?) . . .'

'No go on.'

'OK, because we're just getting to the good bit actually . . .'

That's when he got on to 'personality uploading'.

'What these guys are trying to claim,' said Chuck, 'is that: *What* we are. What holds us together, like memory and motivations, even our body cells, is just a load of data. Arranged in a particular way of course, like some of us get big brains or feet and others just get buck-teeth or big tits. All data, in theory, can be translated into "computer bits". And "bits" can be uploaded. Once uploaded they're not in any real time or space any more. Are you with me?'

'Ye-es.'

'Theoretically, once you're up-loaded you can simply surf through cyber-wonderland and travel to any space or time you choose . . .'

'Hold on a minute. Are you trying to tell me this "Uploading" kick make's things like, say – "time travel" possible?'

'In *theory*, yes.'

'You agree with them then?'

'Yes, in *theory* – even Stephen Hawking is now admitting time travel is *possibly* theoretically possible.'

'He doesn't sound awfully sure.'

'How can anybody be sure. Until someone's done it, I mean. It's only a theory. But quite *possibly* possible . . .'

He was well into his favourite subject now and as he techno-babbled on, I was only half listening.

'. . . provided of course adequate information has been fed into the system – that's a kind of massive job but one that – theoretically – is in no way impossible – once you get self-educating information systems you can speed up that process virtually ad infinitum . . .

But as I said,' he finished. 'Basically it's all a load of bollocks.'

'How can you be so sure?' I countered.

'It's blindingly obvious. Listen, Hawking himself made the point. If time travel were possible, we'd have been invaded by package tours of tourists from the future long ago.'

'Who says the first coachload isn't going to turn up any moment?'

'Maybe they are,' he said with a grin. 'But let's face it, who the hell would want to come here? To the '90's? What have we got to offer? Unemployment, recession, pollution, grid-locked streets – there isn't even anything decent on TV. Let's face it, the '90's must be the Skegness of time-tourism. Given the choice, any self-respecting time traveller would book his ticket to somewhere with a bit more action. Like the French Revolution . . . or the last days of the Roman Empire . . . or when the West was won . . .'

'. . . Or the Sixties,' I suggested suddenly remembering that I was still way behind on research for my Millennium History Project.

'Yeah sure. But it's all a load of bollocks anyway.'

But was it? Whatever Chuck said, it was all starting to make some sort of sense to me. What did a wally like Chuck know about it anyway. Los was on another plane, man.

'So I guess I better get going. Get changed for tonight,' said Chuck when he didn't get any further response from me. 'For Franz's lardy-dardy dress-up-posh affair. That's if my mother's washed my black 501's. Oh Chryst!' he said.

'What?'

'Just remembered where I left them. Do you think Franz will notice if I wear my school trousers?'

'The dreaded Sta-prest Terylenes?'

Chuck nodded miserably.

'Probably not, it's a sit down do . . .'

'But everyone's going to see me, aren't they, when I walk into the restaurant . . .'

'Umm . . .'

'Do you think it matters if I wear trainers?'

'Uh uh . . .'

'Justine?'

'Ummm . . .'

'Maybe I should wear my boxers over my trousers?'

'Umm . . .'

'You're not listening are you?' he said exasperatedly. 'Don't you *care* what I wear?'

I didn't have the heart to tell him that actually I didn't wildly care because I wasn't in fact going to be there.

When Chuck had left, still fussing over what he should or should not put on his lower half for this non-event of the century, I went upstairs and tried on the long black dress.

I stood studying the effect in the bedroom mirror. Geesus, I never realised before what a total lame-head I looked in long dresses. I located a pair of nail scissors and started to attack the skirt. I hacked at it until it had long slits up to mini-length. Where these got out of hand I did a crafty bit of Versace-ing with a packet of safety pins. I was just applying a second coat of puce lipstick – which I gauged was round about the colour TeXas had been wearing – when I heard a ring on the doorbell.

Within a few minutes Henry appeared, breathlessly, in the bedroom doorway.

'Where were you?' she demanded.

'What do you mean?'

'I waited forty-five minutes at Sloane Square. We said we'd go together, remember – to the restaurant?'

Oh my God, it had completely slipped my mind that I was meant to be meeting her.

'I'm so so sorry. I totally forgot.'

'And what the hell have you got on?' Henry continued, staring at me in disbelief.

I did a whirl.

'What do you think?'

'Frankly and honestly?'

'Umm . . .'

'You look like a cross between Mary Poppins and the Wicked Witch of the West.'

'It's my new image.'

'I should say it is. I didn't realise tonight was "fancy dress".'

Henry had on a very short flowered nylon Baby Doll dress and a pink fluffy angora cardigan. She looked like Barbie on a bad day – but since it was the current fashion, I guess she could get away with it.

She took another long assessing look at my outfit.

'Where did you get it – a charity shop?'

'No. It cost a bomb, actually.'

'You're not honestly thinking of wearing that to Franz's party?'

'Actually, no.'

'Then shouldn't you be getting changed?'

'Well, you see the thing is . . .' I was just psyching myself up to tell Henry I wasn't going, when she interrupted:

'Hey. Did you ask that guy?'

'Ask who what?'

'The one you were going to bring to the party?' She was losing patience with me.

'Oh *him*. Umm no.'

'Justine! That means we'll be one male short.'

'No you won't.'

That's when I came clean with her.

'You see, I'm not actually going to to the party . . .'

'You're not?'

I explained about the video.

'You wouldn't expect me to miss an opportunity like this? Would you?'

It seemed she would. Henry then added some pretty outright things about letting friends down and the way I'd changed lately.

As she finished she glanced down.

'Oh my God. What *has* happened to your trainers?'

'I sprayed them.'

'Silver . . . how ghastly,' and then she paused, her eyes widened.

'But they were genuine Caterpillars,' she gasped.

She was really starting to get on my nerves. Henry was typical of a whole generation who basically judged people by the trainers they wore. Honestly they were all *so* immature.

'Look man, I've got to dash,' I said. 'Have a great time tonight.'

'Which reminds me. What about the 60 quid . . . for the dress you trashed. Remember?'

'Bit short of funds at present . . .'

'But you could afford that rag!'

Now she was really bugging me. 'This is for a very important occasion . . .'

'Justine! My mother's going to go bananas.'

'Don't worry about it. It's only money. There are more important things in life.'

'Like what?' demanded Henry.

'You wouldn't understand.'

'Franz is right. You have been really odd lately, Justine,' said Henry shaking her head as she left the room.

'See you round,' she shouted up the stairs.

'Maybe,' I shouted back.

God she was being bo-ring.

I turned and faced myself in the mirror. I think I looked pretty good actually, although I say it myself.

So anyway that's how I happened to find myself in Pratt's Lane Southfields at 10 pm on a Saturday evening.

6

Pratt's Lane is one of those typical South London streets flanked by uniform rows of almond trees, lines of parked cars, and identical semi-detached houses. I walked down the street studying them, becoming more and more convinced that something had gone drastically wrong with my interpretation of the directions. Los couldn't possibly be living here. The area positively reeked of weekend car-washing and DIY.

I studied each house I passed for signs of intelligent life. Basically, the people who lived in them divided into two types – the left-handers whose houses were attached on the right and the right-handers, whose houses were attached on the left. Some time, years ago, some misguided individualist must have had the wild idea of adding a storm porch over their front door to make their house just that little bit different. The idea had passed on down the street like a virus until every house had its own little lopsided lean-to complete with dried out hanging baskets and ailing cacti.

Frankly, this was not at all the kind of environment in which you'd expect to find a world-class group.

But as I approached number 67, I could see an eerie blue light gleaming out through the uncurtained windows.

And as I drew nearer, I heard the deep sexy throb of drumbeats.

I kind of expected a load of limos to be drawn up outside or something. I mean, if they were going to give a concert somewhere, wasn't it about time they hit the road?

I made my way up the crazy-paving path and paused on the front step. I hauled a mirror out of my bag and checked my make-up. Then I took a deep breath and rang on the front doorbell.

It was an *angel chimes* doorbell.

After a few minutes there were footsteps which sounded as if someone was practically falling downstairs and the front door was flung open.

'I didn't think you'd make it,' said Los.

'Why not?' I asked.

He shrugged. 'Thought maybe you'd have something better to do on a Saturday night.'

He was standing in the doorway wearing a black T-shirt that showed off his perfect six-pack. Better to do? Accepting the cheque on a triple roll-over lottery win, maybe? Or being buried alive in an avalanche of Belgian Chocolate Häagen Dazs and having to eat my way out? I defy anyone to think of anything *better* to do.

'So what time does the concert start?' I asked.

'12 G.M.T.,' he said. 'Come on in.'

I followed Los down a bare-boarded hallway that echoed under our feet. He led me up an uncarpeted staircase and past a room whose only furniture appeared to be a load of lumpy looking sleeping bags and a saucer piled with cigarette buts.

The stairwell was lit by a single naked bulb and as we passed what I took to be the bathroom, I caught a glimpse of a stained avocado suite, circa 1950 brown and orange flowered tiling, and a decaying ali-baba linen basket. Apart from that, the house was totally empty save for acres of icy linoleum and walls fluttering with tattered wallpaper.

Number 67 Pratt's Lane was a squat.

We continued past the first floor and went up a set of rickety steps into the loft.

The loft didn't look at all like a loft once you were in it. It looked more like a set from a sci-fi movie.

Basically, the whole area appeared to have been lined with crushed silver foil. By the light of a single blue bulb I could see Phil and TeXas crouched over a load of equipment.

Phil disentangled a tripod and started making a lot of fuss about getting it in the right position and taking some test footage.

Los gestured that I should find somewhere to settle and I selected what looked like a cushion and turned out to be a pile of old clothes.

Half an hour passed and it became clear that Los was getting impatient. He was fidgeting around and making popping noises on the microphone.

Phil switched on some really bright lights and TeXas stood peering through a camera lens at him. A small monitor fizzed with static. As it settled Phil appeared in the centre of the screen.

'That's OK, fine. Now we can use Justine.'

'So what do I have to do?' I asked.

I was instructed to sit on a chair and look into the camera lens.

TeXas cast a searching look across my face and dusted it with some powder.

The monitor fizzed again and then a video of a starscape started to come up.

'Ready?' asked TeXas and she turned the camera on to me.

I saw my own face superimposed across the starscape. This cut to the rings of Saturn and then to some footage that looked like the surface of another planet. I guess, because I'm blonde and fairly pale-skinned my face kind of bleached out and blended in as if it was part of the landscape. It was a sensational effect.

Phil had started playing around on the drums. Los seated himself at a keyboard. TeXas played a few chords on the guitar.

'But what about the concert?' I asked.

'Just ten minutes to go,' said Phil looking at his watch.

'It's a worldwide gig tonight,' explained Los.

Nobody seemed on the point of getting up and going anywhere.

'Shouldn't we be making a move then?' I asked.

'The gig's here,' said Los.

'Here?' I asked incredulously. (This wasn't exactly Wembley Stadium.)

Los pointed to a telephone socket in the wall.

'That is linking us in to a potential world audience of billions – difficult to assess how many precisely – of course.'

'But where are they?'

Phil pulled a plug from out of a socket and held it towards me with an expression that told me in no uncertain terms that I was about the biggest lame-head that ever drew breath.

'At the other end of this. This links us into the Net.'

'It's a *live* gig,' said TeXas.

'That's the point of cyber-busking,' said Los. 'We play to any geeks who have access. It's up to the fans to pick us up. For certain there's a load of them in SoHo, L.A.'s a big audience, and maybe Rio. In Sydney there are some guys who look in. And who knows who else?'

'So the concert's worldwide *on the Net*.'

'Sure, what did you think?'

'I don't know what I thought.'

'Music's live, as are the visual mixes. All digital – a total live multi-media experience.'

Geesus! I thought. Here I was, technologically challenged me – the star of a worldwide multi-media experience! I sat there glued to my chair with the camera focused on me – as mystified as a monkey on a moon mission, hardly daring to breathe.

At precisely midnight, the group started up with a mind-blowing burst of sound.

OK, so you want to know what the music was like?

The first number was all electronic. Basically, it sounded as if they'd recorded sounds from virtually anything, car alarms, clocks ticking, even something that sounded like bathwater going down a plughole. Then they'd multiplied it and mixed it and scratched it until the sounds that came out were like nothing I had ever heard before. Techno was putting it mildly!

After that TeXas sang a number called 'Deep Blue' and she had a really rich, velvety voice, I would have given anything to sing like that.

And then Los sang. It was a song called 'Silver Surfer'. The lyrics were about the kind of people you met on the Net – quite a wacky lot by the sound of them – they all had made-up names like Snoopy Dog and Choc-Drops and The Grim Reaper. But there was a guy in the song who had fallen in love with a girl called Venus. And they'd really hit it off and then he'd discovered that she lived ten thousand light years away in another time-span and she was sending him messages through aeons of dataspace. There was no way they could ever end up together in reality. It was so-oo sad. It really got to me. Honestly, I had this lump in my throat the size of a golf ball and it just wouldn't go away. I could feel my eyes were positively oozing. God, I felt such a wally!

When the song came to an end, Los nodded and whispered to me, 'Cool. Just what we wanted.'

After that, Los played a keyboard number which was all instrumental – if you could call it that. It was based on something I recognised. An old Beatles' number that I remembered because it had a really odd name, 'Magical Mystery Tour'. I always used to think this sounded like the most awesome and fascinating trip you could imagine. And then I found out the title referred to a bus-load of oldies going on a day's outing to the seaside. I wondered if these guys had any idea what the song was about. All this 'lateral thinking' gave me time to recover. So by the time the music finished I was looking more or less presentable.

Later, when the gig had come to an end, we all sat around kind of flaked out. And I actually started to feel that I fitted in. I was one of them. We'd shared in a never-to-be-repeated experience, performed together on a worldwide scale. But it was more than that . . .

Up until now, as a kid at school and with friends I'd made through the accident of where I lived, or who went to my school, I'd kind of got roped in and had to conform to a pattern to fit in. But here, for the first time in my life I was with people who were from way outside my world. They had extended its boundaries, made my world larger somehow. And although they were older, and had obviously been around a hell of a lot more than me, they actually seemed to accept me.

We didn't talk much. Los put some music on and we just chilled out on the floor. Phil made some coffee and they all smoked like mad.

'Say, has anyone heard from those guys about the album?' asked TeXas eventually.

'What album?' I asked, feeling really guilty

'Some big fish interested in an album deal,' said Phil.

'Spielberg,' said Los.

'Really?'

'Want to meet up IRL.'

'Haven't heard from them yet though.'

'I guess these things take time,' I said. And then I had a sudden thought. 'Talking of time, what is the time?'

Phil ripped a sheet of silver foil back from a skylight.

'Must be nearly 5 am,' he said, peering through it.

'Oh no.' It was true. We were blinking in the early morning light. Time had gone by so fast. It just couldn't be dawn already.

'I've got to go,' I said.

'Too early for the first Tube,' said Los.

'It's OK, I'll walk,' I said.

'I'll walk with you,' said Los.

TeXas gave him a meaningful look.

But he ignored her and grabbed his mac and swung it over his shoulder.

'Come on, let's go,' he said.

And I followed him down the stairs – or rather glided. He wanted to walk me home!

We made our way past the silent houses. We walked for ages through the still suburbs and found our way down to the Thames. Dawn was breaking in a kind of pinky grey haze over the river. It was just so-so-oo romantic.

It didn't strike me till later, but I guess on that walk I was the one who did most of the talking. You know how you do when you don't want to have an awkward silence on your hands? And Los was a good listener, really interested in all the trivial details of my life. But looking back on it now, I realise I didn't learn much about him. He was really odd about talking about himself. Even a totally ordinary question like 'where did his parents live' or 'where he'd gone to school' and he'd kind of clam up on me.

We paused on Putney Bridge and looked down into the water. And then we turned to each other at precisely the same moment. Look, you're not going to believe this because this sort of thing never happens to me. I mean, it does with really gross boys who are too drunk or too short or not my type at all. But it never does with the kind of absolutely fit and delectable guy that Los was. He leaned towards me and brushed my hair back from my face . . . And kissed me.

It was a long, slow, meaningful kiss.

I'm absolutely positive that this was the most poignant moment of my whole entire life. Even if I live to ninety-five, I'm never going to experience anything anywhere near like it again.

But afterwards he swung round, turning away from me.

'I shouldn't've done that,' he said. He stood hunched against the rail staring down into the water.

'Yes, you should've,' I said.

'No – you don't understand.'

'Is there someone else?'

He shook his head.

'There must be.'

(No one this gorgeous could be actually out on the loose and up for grabs.) 'It's TeXas isn't it?'

'No. It's not TeXas. It's not anybody.'

'Then what's the problem?'

'It's just that we're from different . . . different . . .' he paused looking at me in an agonised way.

Oh my God, it was one of those 'rich girl meets poor boy' situations.

'Because I'm a "spoilt brat",' I said making light of it. 'None of that matters to me.'

He shook his head again.

'It's a lot more complicated than that.'

'Then what?'

'You wouldn't believe me if I told you . . .'

'Try me.'

'Let's walk,' he said.

And as we walked he came out with this *load of total garbage*.

I mean, if a guy actually doesn't fancy you he should say so right out. I could take it. Just. But he didn't have to fabricate such a ridiculous and crazy excuse. I mean I may look dumb at times but frankly what did he take me for?

'Wouldn't it be simpler to say you really don't fancy me at all?'

'But that's the trouble, I do.'

We walked back in a kind of numb mutual silence. It wasn't until we arrived at 122 Cheyne Walk that the spell was broken.

The time of our arrival coincided most unfortunately with the precise moment Caroline came outside to put the rubbish in the dustbins. And if seeing my mother in a dressing gown and slippers with a dustbin liner in her hand doesn't bring you down to earth with a jolt, I don't know what would.

It's difficult to do justice in words to the look of intense horror that came over her face and seemed to work its way down and through her entire body when she saw Los.

'Justine!' she said. 'What do you think you are doing coming home at this hour?'

Los stepped forward. 'Now let's all cool it. I think I can explain,' he started.

Caroline was so enraged she only caught a few odd words which most unfortunately were things like 'gig' and 'video' which, if anything, served to make her even more incensed.

I was ordered inside and the door was firmly closed in Los's face.

'That was just so rude!' I protested.

'Rude!' started Caroline. The tirade raged for at least half an hour and spread to include Daddy, who had appeared at the top of the stairs with his face covered in shaving foam.

'So what were you doing all night?' demanded Caroline, her eyes blazing.

'Precisely what we said. Making a video. And don't look like that. We were all fully dressed – all the time!'

This prompted another burst of fury from her.

'You know what the trouble with you is – you think our generation is just as sex-obsessed as yours. We all know what you lot got up to in the Sixties.'

Daddy joined in at that point and I was told in no uncertain terms that appalling behaviour like staying-out-all-night – even if we spent the whole night playing Monopoly – which he doubted – was not to be tolerated.

You know, it's sad in its way. What parents seem to have forgotten – and maybe this is because all that falling-in-love stuff is such a dim distant memory for them – is what it's like to be young. What it's like to be at the beginning of everything and not old and disillusioned like them. What they've forgotten is that basically we all have our own set of rules. Mine are:

Rule one: Don't make the first move in case you're rejected.

Rule two: If he makes the first move – don't seem too keen or he'll probably think you're *anyone's*.

Rule three: Take things *really* slowly – This way at least you postpone the disillusionment of finding out you weren't meant for each other anyway.

But who can explain that to parents?

Anyway, the net effect of all this 'totally unacceptable behaviour' was that I was grounded indefinitely, with a total shut-down on funds and I was forbidden to see 'that frightful person' ever again.

7

You know how when you're a kid you kind of write your personal address in new exercise books and things like this:

Justine Duval
Third floor front bedroom
122 Cheyne Walk
Chelsea
London SW10
England
The British Isles
Europe
The Northern Hemisphere
The World
The Solar System
The Milky Way
The Galaxy
The Universe
Infinity
Beyond
Etc.

. . . and you think, that's where you are, with everything going on round you. You are dead-centre and it all kind of splays off on all sides until it gets to whatever there is beyond the end of everything. Well, ever since I could remember, I'd felt like that. Parents moved round me like great friendly planets in orbit. Countries like Finland were aeons away. And India and Africa light years beyond. Of course, my universe got bigger as I moved on to school and made friends etc. But basically, I was always at the centre where the action is. Well, suddenly I didn't feel like that any more. Since I'd met Los it was as if I had taken this massive step to the side. This may sound really odd but it wasn't me at the dead centre of the universe any more. It was *him*. I guess this must be what people call *love*.

And there's another thing. When I was a child I used to think that my parents knew everything. They were just kind of large looming godlike presences stored with an infinite supply of wisdom. As I grew larger I started to doubt whether they were quite as wise as they liked to pretend. In my new adult status, I now realised that they were barely scraping the surface. In fact, I was starting to question whether they knew *anything*. I mean, look at their attitude to Los?

I had been forbidden to see him or to speak to him. But it hadn't occurred to them there were other ways of communicating: I e-mailed him straight away.

S.O.S.
Held prisoner by evil forces
at 122 Cheyne Walk
Contact forbidden IRL
Advise please

But Los obviously wasn't anywhere near his computer so I didn't get an answer.

Actually, that day I don't think I was getting through to anyone.

Franz rang at around lunchtime.

'Thanks a lot for the card and the fabulous birthday present and for being the life and soul of the party last night,' she said.

'Oh, Fran darling, I'm so, so sorry, I'll make it up to you, I promise.'

'I'm expecting to hear that you broke both legs, or got arrested for running a "girl-gang" – or spent the evening bound and gagged and tied to the bedpost by a masked intruder, at least.'

'Yeah all of those, only *worse*.'

'Out with it . . .'

'I'm in love.'

'Ahhh . . .'

'Am I forgiven?'

'So what's *worse* about it?'

'He doesn't love me. Or at least he does, I know he does but he doesn't want to.'

'Well, I don't blame him, frankly. I wouldn't want to be in love with you, Justine. You are a selfish cow at times – especially last night.'

'Oh God, I know.'

'Glad to hear it.'

There was a pause. I blew my nose on a tissue.

'Don't tell me you're expecting me to come over all Agony Aunt for you?'

'Don't think there's much advice you can give me on this one.'

There was a sigh. 'So what's the problem?'

'You sitting down?'

'Sure. Shoot.'

'Well . . .' (How did one start?) 'Basically, we're too different.'

'Opposites are meant to attract.'

'We're from totally different backgrounds.'

'Look at Imran Khan and Jemima Goldsmith.'

'You don't understand. He's from a different time-span.'

'What's he . . . geriatric or something?'

'No, it's not his age, it's where he's from.'

'Like . . . Tonbridge Wells?'

'Further than that . . .'

'. . . Torquay?'

I took a deep breath.

'Basically, a long term relationship is out of the question.'

'Why?'

I swallowed. 'He says he's from the future. He's a time traveller . . .'

There was a shriek of hilarity the other end.

'Well at least he's original!'

'He says that people who live where he comes from don't believe in one-to-one relationships, that's mere selfish possessiveness and politically incorrect.'

'OK, correction! Not so original after all. Guys like him have been giving us that line since the beginning of time!'

'I don't know whether to believe him or not.'

'Justine! You are seriously losing the plot over this one. Geesus, a time traveller! Can't you see he's sending you up?'

'Yeah, I guess you're right. I mean, I know you're right. Geesus, I've made such a fool of myself.'

Franz made sympathetic noises the other end and suggested that we met up later for a coffee.

'I'm not actually allowed out.'

'No . . . why?'

'Mummy caught us coming back at breakfast time this morning.'

'Justine. You didn't! You couldn't've . . . Not with a creature from outa-time! (Another most uncalled for shriek of merriment.) Did you?'

'I wish . . .' I said.

Some twenty minutes later Henry called.

'Franz has just informed me you've come totally off your trolley.'

(Henry is the scientific one among us.)

'You don't sound very sympathetic.'

'I'm not.'

'You could at least humour me.'

'When are you going to crack out of this?'

'You just don't understand, he's just so so gorgeous.'

'That's what you said about all the others.'

'But it's different this time. This time – it's Love.'

'Forgive me for remembering, but that's also what you said about the others.'

'I knew you wouldn't understand.'

'Justine. Wise up, please, can't you?'

Chuck didn't ring. But when I went into Daddy's study I found this little e-mail message waiting for me:

To: JD
From: http://www.cnd.com
Hear you're feeling . . .
:-(
Don't
:'-(
Hope you'll be
:-)
real soon.
(To read smileys, turn head on one side)

Chuck, what would I do without you? If you weren't such a total dweeb I swear I could almost fall for you. Sigh.

I spent the afternoon slumped on the sofa with the TV remote control, flicking idly through mass-market 'infotainment' and generating vibes of discontent in a parental direction.

I considered various avenues of vengeance, such as ordering a hundred or so 'Lovers by Post' albums on Daddy's credit card. Or sending for a starter pack and signing Mummy up as a Cabouchard Giltware representative. Or phoning the Australian speaking clock and leaving the receiver off the hook. But I guessed in the long run any of these things would be more than likely to make the situation worse.

My jailors were watching my every move. Caroline had even taken a 'tablet' she'd found at the bottom of my schoolbag to be analysed. She was livid when she discovered it was only a Peppermint Tic-Tac and was charged for this information.

I tried demonstrating my resistence with a big silent act of *not eating anything.* At mealtimes Caroline and Daddy made loud cheerful conversation between themselves as if I were part of the furniture. And on Saturday night Caroline served up my favourite dinner. God what it is to suffer!

By bedtime I was so starving, I had to do a fridge raid. I was just heading back past Daddy's study with a loaded tray when I thought I'd have a last check on the computer again.

There it was. An e-mail for me.

I recognised it. It was a verse from 'Silver Surfer'. It read:

VENUS
brightest star on my horizon
(This was the good bit)
A billion billion stars
Shine in my heart
While a billion billion hours
Keep us apart

OK, for a put-down it was poetic, I give him that.

But he didn't expect me to give up there did he? I mean, he'd more or less admitted he was hooked. Brightest star on my horizon, I thought contentedly as I went up to bed. I'd call that pretty positive actually.

Next morning – still nurturing what was left of that positive attitude – I decided that the only cure for lovesickness was to find something worse. I was going to devote some quality time to my long overdue Millennium History Project. I figured a bit of 'serious application' might help with the parental situation as well. Even though I was currently doing everything in my power to bring them round, I wasn't getting anywhere.

Actually, it was fortunate that I decided to get down to it at that point, because, although I'd had a whole year to work on it, I discovered that it was meant to be handed in, *in two days time*. And my Millenium Project was going to be a real masterpiece, with masses of visuals and graphics and arty changes of typeface done on Daddy's computer.

I had collected a pretty impressive stock of 'prime source material'. There was quite a lot of real original Sixties stuff stashed away in odd corners of the house. There were photos, of course, horrendous ones of Daddy in flares with hair sleeked down on top and reappearing greasily somewhere beneath his ears, and Mummy peering out through ink-black panda-eyes fringed with false lashes.

A raid on Daddy's secrets drawer had yielded some real gems – a whole stash of pre-decimalisation notes and coins and a *Daily Telegraph* from July 1967 that contained an announcement of the 'Coming of Age' of Hannah –

Caroline's elder sister – the one who went totally off the rails and ended up collecting cats.

In Caroline's cupboard I had found a genuine Biba silver sheath dress with cut-away armholes and in the inner pocket of an old handbag there was a little cardboard rail ticket to Little Walping – the nearest station to 'Trudgings', Grampy's Norfolk home.

I had been keeping all these in a shoebox and I spent the entire morning scanning anything scannable in with Daddy's high-resolution colour scanner. All this 'fascinating original visual material' had taken up pages and pages – which hardly left any room in between for writing boring text, which was a bit of a bonus really.

Daddy had popped in a few times to see how I was getting on. On his first visit he made surprised and approving noises. On his second, he asked a few naive and predictable questions. On the third, he made use of this newly acquired knowledge. He was giving some Sunday lunch guests a guided tour of his little grey plastic empire. I was trying to concentrate on my project and only caught snatches of his blatant showing off.

'. . . Any information I want to get right here, at my desk – devilishly ingenious . . .'

'. . . Everything I need – scanner,' he said pointing to the printer. 'Modem,' pointing to the scanner. 'Genius of modern technology eh? Course it's the way the world's going – can't keep on cutting down rainforests and carting them round the world, can we? Get on the Information Superhighway, that's what I say . . . In the fast lane, eh? (Guffaw, guffaw.)'

And all this from someone who still couldn't look up his share prices without the aid of written instructions on a scrap of exercise book. Sad case.

At intervals, in between working, I tried e-mailing Los. But each time I got the bald message:

Sorry
AFK

I rang Chuck.

'Who the hell is AFK?' I asked.

'Long-lost relation of JFK?' he suggested.

'Unlikely to be using Los's computer.'

'You didn't find it on an e-mail by any chance?'

'How did you guess?'

'AFK,' said Chuck with a sigh, 'is a TLA meaning "Away From Keyboard".'

Well that was a bit of a bummer. Where was he? I wondered.

By four that afternoon I had finished all the scanning and was deliberating on how I should 'Save' my day's work.

These important deliberations were interrupted by my mother's voice.

'Justine!' she appeared in the doorway with a teatowel in her hand. 'I've just had Henrietta's mother on the phone . . .'

'Umm.' (Maybe I should try 'Save as'.)

'I thought I gave you the money for the dress of Henrietta's you ruined?'

'Ahhh . . .' (Or maybe just 'Save'.)

'What did you do with it then?'

'Well, you know that black dress of mine . . .' (Or maybe I should select 'Quit' first and then 'Save' it.)

'That ghastly black hag outfit?'

'Ummm.'

'But you couldn't have spent £60 on a ripped rag.'

'It wasn't ripped when I bought it.'

'Justine, how many times have I told you about mutilating your clothes . . .'

'Geesus, can you just let me concentrate for a minute?'

I selected 'Quit' and the screen went blank.

I reselected 'Millennium Project'. *It wasn't there!* That was hours and hours of painstaking work. I searched frantically and fruitlessly through other files. Geesus, I don't believe this!

'Now look what you've done!' I raged at her.

'Justine. *I* haven't *done* anything.'

'Yes you have, you've distracted me. And now I've lost a whole day's work and I'm going to have to start right back at the beginning – that's what you've done.'

My mother stood in the doorway and took the full force of my impotent rage.

'I don't know why your father bought the beastly thing . . .' she said, gazing at the computer as if it were some expensive and totally uncontrollable family pet – a rogue rottweiler or something.

'So what's she done now . . . ?' my father joined her. He caught sight of the blank screen. 'Oh no, not again . . .'

I made a quick dodge for the front door before a classic parental tirade could begin.

I just had to get out of the *home atmosphere* before I died of suffocation.

As the front door slammed behind me a futile final bellow came from above.

'And Justine . . . remember, you are grounded. You are not going anywhere!'

I steamed down the road.

Who does she think she is? Here I am. A person fully grown to my full height and hopefully weight. I'm sixteen, old enough to have wild flings without being prosecuted. Old enough to get married without asking her opinion even. *Have babies*, if I were crazy or careless enough. Legally entitled to leave school and get a job. And she still treats me like a child! It's as if she thinks she owns me.

I stormed on taking very little notice of where I was going. I walked miles! At least right down the King's Road and across Eel Brook Common. I had to find some way of proving in a meaningful and *permanent* way that I was my own person. Something that was painful and took courage and that could not be ignored. I turned into the Fulham Road.

That's when I saw the sign:

Archie Art Tattooist.
Original Designs in Vivid Colour.
Customised Designs to Order.
New needles for each client.
Enquire within.

I stood for some minutes outside. Something permanent and irreversible and meaningful . . .

I pushed open the door and walked in. There was a waiting room like a dentist's and a desk with a bell on it. I rang the bell with determination. A man in a singlet leaned out of a further doorway. He was drying his hands on a towel and as he did so, a massive python appeared to writhe up and down the muscles of his arm.

'Hang on a min. What can I do you for?'

'Are you Archie?'

'Be with you in a mo', luv.' He leaned back into the room and I heard money change hands.

'Same time next week?' he said.

A massive bloke built like a wrestler strode past. He had half a naked lady on his upper arm.

'Well then?' said Archie.

'I'd like a tattoo,' I said. 'Just a small one.'

Archie looked at me doubtfully. 'How old are you, luv?'

'Eighteen,' I lied.

'Got ID?' he asked.

'Not on me.'

He looked even more doubtful.

'Tattoos is permanent,' he said. 'No good you coming back when it's done like and saying as you've changed your mind. They're there for good 'n all.'

'I know,' I said. 'That's why I want it done.'

'Your mum know you're doing this?'

A vision of my mother's affronted face rose before my eyes. If anything it heightened my determination.

'I haven't got a mum. I live with this witch called Caroline,' I said.

'Like that is it?' said Archie.

I nodded.

'Well, what did you have in mind then? Nice little red heart? A rosebud? I do a lovely cherub, that's popular with the ladies.'

'Have you got a bit of paper?'

He handed me a grubby pad and a biro. I wrote the letters:

I L O V E. L O S

He looked unimpressed.

'I could do you something a bit more artistic than that,' he said. He opened a greasy looking colour brochure and showed me some big colourful fairground-style letters.

'No, it's got to be just like that. Nothing fancy.'

He looked truly upset. As if I was criticising his artistic judgement.

'But what about the colour?' he asked.

'No. Just black'll be fine.'

He shook his head doubtfully.

'Colour don't cost no more,' he said.

Anyway, after a lot of persuasion, Archie agreed to do the tattoo.

He made me sit down for five minutes to think about it. In case I changed my mind. But I didn't change my mind. Five minutes of considering all that pain and suffering actually reinforced my resolution. I won't go into the actual ordeal. It was agony. And I'm a total physical coward. I mean, I think I feel pain far more than other people. Which is what made it so-oo much more significant.

I left Archie's place with the tattoo smarting dreadfully. And I spent the next day wishing I'd chosen some other place to have it done. Sitting down was pure hell.

But frankly, this was nothing compared to the mental anguish I was suffering. It went something like this: You meet someone and it seems to you that the world's taken off on a different plane. Colours are brighter. Pavements have a bounce to them. Birds are tweeting ferociously joyfully from every twig. Your favourite tunes are being played in all the shops. To top it all he thinks you're pretty delicious too. Couldn't be better. But fate always has that inevitable killjoy attitude when things are going too much your way, hasn't it? He'd disappeared. As far as I was concerned he might well have dematerialised into thin air.

I'd e-mailed and e-mailed and e-mailed – but I always got the same dumb reply:

Sorry
AFK

And then, when I was at my lowest ebb, my mother discovered about the tattoo. I won't bore you with the whole scene but it included phrases like 'mutilating your body', 'risking Aids and God-knows-what-else', 'looking like a navvy for the rest of your life', all working up to the usual finale 'quite frankly Justine, sometimes I wonder where I went wrong.'

The upshot of all this was that I packed a small bag with my toothbrush and Fred Bear and headed for number 67 Pratts Lane and a new life.

8

I rang the front doorbell of number 67 Pratt's Lane.

There were several tense seconds of breathless waiting while I strained my ears for the sound of footsteps descending the stairs. Nothing happened.

I rang again – harder this time. There was still no response. Where were they? I moved round to the window and peered through, there was no-one in the front room.

Pushing open the rotting side gate, I picked my way over a pile of rubbish to the backdoor. I knocked hard on that. Still no response. I tried the door handle. The door wasn't locked. It slid open.

A pile of food-encrusted crockery lay in the sink. There was a milk bottle with sour milk congealing at the top. It didn't look as if anyone had been there in days.

'Hallo,' I called. My voice echoed hollowly through the unfurnished house.

I tiptoed down the hallway.

'Anyone at home?'

I could hear a tapping noise from above.

'Hello, it's me, Justine.' I made my way up the stairs, hoping . . .

In the bedroom the bit of fabric that served as a curtain was catching in the breeze. Behind it was a broken pane of glass. I'd never seen a room look so empty. Los's bedroll was rolled up in one corner and a mug of cold congealed tea was beside it. Apart from that, there was nothing except the bare floorboards.

I could feel a big lump in my throat and tears welling up in my eyes. I swallowed. I hadn't tried the loft yet. The loft was probably soundproofed. There was still a chance . . .

The loft was also cold, bare and empty. No signs of life there either. Except . . . Wait a minute . . . The computer . . . For some reason that had been left on . . .

I was well-trained in electrical appliances. Whenever we went away they were not only turned off, but 'plugs out' was Daddy's rule. I think he had a theory that if they weren't, all our electrical appliances would have some sort of wild party, running up massive bills while we weren't there.

In a highly responsible manner, I went over to the computer to turn it off. Hang on, it had a message on it. It read:

GONE SURFING

To upload use password:
SERENDIPITY?
:-)
BCNU
LA

Select Y to proceed N to return to main menu.
Y N

Surfing! Where for Godsake? BCNU? . . . BCNU? Suddenly the penny dropped. Be seein' you.. L A. Los Angeles . . . But where?

There was only one way to find out. I sat at the screen and typed in 'Y'. A message flashed up:

DO YOU WISH TO UPLOAD?
Select Y to proceed N to return to main menu.
Y N

Upload? Did I wish to upload? Sounded dodgy. But on the other hand what was the point of going back to the beginning? So I took a deep breath and selected 'Y' again. This was followed by what seemed like an age of acute electronic indigestion. When the crackling and whirring ended an 'Error Message' came up.

WARNING
Access restricted
To Proceed Type in Password:..............
with the options:
Cancel Continue

I took another, deeper breath and typed SERENDIPITY? and selected 'Continue'.

There was even more violent crackling and whirring and the screen glitched all over. Then it settled to a pure glowing white with the stark message:

WARNING
REPEAT
UPLOADING PROCEDURE IS UNDOABLE

DO YOU STILL WISH TO CONTINUE?
Select Y to proceed N to return to main menu.
Y N

Of course I wished to continue. Geesus, what a fuss about a silly old procedure. I selected 'Y' again.

At that point a picture started to come up. It scrolled and cleared. Glitched. Then scrolled and cleared again. HELLO. That was me on screen wasn't it? As if a camera was trained on me. Behind my image I could see a grid of white light. Another message rolled up:

CAUTION
UPLOADING IN PROGRESS
THIS PROCEDURE CANNOT BE INTERRUPTED

At this point one of those dear little clock things started whizzing round and round like nobody's business. A simply horrendous static fizzing noise filled the room. Then this vast blinking exclamation mark came up on the screen and the computer started making convulsive 'I am about to explode' noises. Jagged beams like lightning started to flash out from the monitor.

I knew it. Just my luck! As a reflex action, I leant down and pulled the plug out of the wall.

The screen went totally blank.

All I could see was the positive and then the negative image of the lightning gleaming, red and then green, in my eyes. These cleared and . . . Hang on a minute . . . What had happened to the room?

I swung round. The room wasn't a room any more, it was a great grid of light. White bands on green. I took a step forward and put out a hand to touch something solid and familiar. There wasn't anything solid or remotely familiar. *Not even the walls. They weren't there any more . . .*

Boy! Geesus. OMG! Chryst!

Pull yourself together, Justine. These things just don't happen.

Take a deep breath. Count to ten. Pinch yourself. Close your eyes and open them again . . .

It was still there!

I was in the Net.

I looked warily around me. As my eyes grew accustomed to the dazzling light, I could see that the squares of the grid were labelled, with little white electronic letters – like drawers in a filing cabinet. I started to read the labels on the ones nearest me.

Alabaster . . . Albatross . . . Albinoni . . .

OK, so they were in alphabetical order. Big Deal! So if this was the Net, it confirmed everything I'd ever thought. It was an environment that, by the look of it, had all the mind-blowing thrills of the Concise Oxford Dictionary. Could this be what people called *surfing*? It was more like being accidentally locked into some great electronic reference library.

And where was Los? Where was anyone, in fact? Where was the way out? Was there a way out? With a horrible sinking feeling I wondered what I had got myself into. I scanned further round the room, searching for inspiration. I came to the D's.

There was a drawer with my name on it:

Duval – Justine

Freaky! The drawer hadn't been closed properly. I peeped inside. There it was – my precious 'history project' – everything I had scanned in. I hadn't wiped it after all. It was packed in a neat transparent plastic folder, marked as I'd labelled it:

Millennium Project

I looked inside – there was the pre-decimalisation cash, the *Daily Telegraph* and the contents of Caroline's old handbag – I lifted the folder out.

So what should I do now? I searched around the Net for clues. That was when I noticed a little flashing shape. It was lit up like an icon – a rectangle flanked by columns and topped by a triangle – the shape of a doorway. As I drew closer it grew larger and larger. Maybe it was a doorway. It had the number 67 written on it. It almost looked real. I put out my hand to touch it. And it swung open.

Through it, there was a crazy – paving path leading down to the peeling wooden gate. I stared even harder. This doorway seemed to lead out of the Net and back into reality.

I walked gingerly through the door and sure enough found myself standing outside 67 Pratt's Lane, back *in the real world*. Phew! That was a relief! My first attempt at surfing – short but sweet! But what the hell! I was only a beginner, wasn't I?

I was just congratulating myself at handling the situation pretty well actually, when I heard the front door of the house slam behind me.

I swung round and stood stupidly staring at it wondering what to do next. Maybe Los was inside after all! I peered through the letterbox but the house was as deserted as ever. It must have been the wind.

That's when everything got to me. Where was Los? He could be *anywhere*. I resolved there and then, that even if I had to scour the entire planet, I was going to find him. How far could a girl go without losing her self-respect? OK – to hell with self-respect – with a guy this horny, who cares? But finding him could take time, and currently what choice did I have but to go home and face further parental fury?

Honestly, I hadn't felt this dejected since . . . since . . .

I couldn't even think of a time to compare it with, it was that bad.

A taxi happened to be heading down the street at that moment. In a reflex action I hailed it and climbed inside.

'Where to, luv?'

'122 Cheyne Walk,' I said miserably.

I had a good cry in the taxi actually. By the time it drew up outside my house I could feel my face had gone all hot and blotchy.

'That'll be eight and six,' said the cabbie.

Eight and six, what was he talking about? Eight pounds sixty?

Which is when I remembered I hadn't any money, still I supposed I could get some off Caroline.

'Do you mind hanging on a minute. I'll have to go inside to get you some cash.'

I rang on the doorbell. As I did so I noticed something very very odd indeed . . .

The front door had changed colour.

I swung round to check whether I had somehow walked up to the wrong house. Then the front door opened and I was confronted by someone I had never seen before. Instead of Caroline, an extremely large lady in a frilled floral apron was standing in our hallway as if she owned the place.

'Yes?' she said.

I gazed past her to find that our wall-to-wall eau de nil Axminster had been replaced by worn brown parquet pattern linoleum with a moth-eaten floral runner positioned down the centre.

'Well?' said the woman.

'I think,' I stammered as I took in the general impression of the hallway – brown linoleum, embossed lime and cream wallpaper, musty air, a lurid print of a blue faced lady on the wall, a set of coat hooks made like notes on a stave – all accompanied by the lugubrious ticking of a sunburst wall clock. Nightmare!

'I think I must have the wrong house,' I stammered.

'Which house was it you was wanting?' she asked.

'Number 122? The Duvals?'

'This is number 122. No one of that name here,' she said.

'But it can't be, there must be some mistake . . .' I said, standing staring at her like an idiot.

'Your mistake not mine,' she said as she shut the door in my face and sure enough I saw that, in place of my parents' nice thick brass numbers, the number 122 was screwed to the door in white plastic letters.

But it wasn't the wrong house. It had the same steps and gate and everything . . .

The cabbie had got out of his cab and was standing on the pavement.

'What seems to be the problem?' he asked.

An innocent question in itself, but a tricky one to answer. A number of responses crossed my mind like: A mad woman seems to have moved into my house and changed all the decor. I'm having an extremely long and convoluted dream, please wake me up. Or, hang on a minute while I scream, I've gone stark raving bonkers.

Instead I said, 'I don't seem to have any money on me.'

The cabbie looked most affronted at this. He pointed at the transparent folder and said, 'What's that in there then?'

I stood there limply while he took the folder from me, extricated a brown note with Ten shillings written on it and counted out some change.

'And a tanner tip, thank you very much indeed, I must say,' he said and huffily climbed back in the cab and drove off.

I was left standing staring at the house. It *was* my house. Except the paint on the front door wasn't black any more, it was sickly olive green. It *couldn't* be the wrong house. There was number 123 on one side and number 121 on the other. And it wasn't the wrong street either, because there was the Thames on the other side of the road with all the houseboats on it. I even walked down to the corner to check that the sign at the end of the street said 'Cheyne Walk'.

But something really strange had happened. I tried to place precisely what was different. The cars for a start. They looked like something out of an old 'Carry On' movie. Instead of the standard Cheyne Walk BMW's and Mercedes Jeeps, the ones parked were all oddly out of date.

Maybe there was some kind of old car rally going on in the street? Or they were making a film perhaps? That was it! A film crew had set all this up to shoot a re-make of *Genevieve* or something, and they'd resprayed my front door – the woman in the floral apron was an actress . . .

I walked slowly up Cheyne Walk trying to make this scenario fit with what my senses were telling me.

A few hunded yards further on, this theory was well and truly disproved. The Pagoda, which my parents had always called 'that abomination', and which had been built in Battersea Park some ten or so years ago, and was a huge – a positively unmissable landmark – wasn't there any longer . . . No one could have moved that. Then, a little further on, in the distance, from the chimneys of Battersea Power Station, which had been in ruins for as long as I could remember – I saw four columns of smoke rising. It was back in service.

I continued on my way to Sloane Square feeling rather weak at the knees. Well, good old familiar Sloane Square tube station and dear old drab Peter Jones were there all right, looking just as dated as ever. In front of the tube station was a newspaper seller.

I picked up a *Times*.

The date on it read: 29 July 1967. *Nineteen sixty seven*!

That was thirty years in the past!

Oh . . . my . . . God!

Geesus!

Chryst almighty!

9

The worst thing about being flung in such a random manner into another age, was having to admit that the *impossible* was possible. My brain tried every turn and twist to make sense of the whole thing and to reject the totally unacceptable idea that I, Justine Duval, ordinary citizen of 1997, had actually *travelled back through time*.

I realised then, with sudden mind-blowing clarity, that Los hadn't been having me on. He'd been deadly serious all the time. All that time-travel stuff that Chuck and Franz and Henry had claimed was teasing and taunting and sending me up, hadn't been a joke at all. That explained where he disappeared to all the time. Why he was never around. He was surfing – uploaded somewhere in the Net, but where? Where was he now?

I stared blankly in the direction of the Royal Court Theatre, trying to come to terms with this sudden and most disconcerting turn of events.

Saved was the name of the play currently being performed. And there was a disclaimer pasted across the poster, which read: 'Banned by the Lord Chamberlain'.

'You going to buy that paper, ducks? This ain't no public

library,' the newspaper seller was addressing me.

I reached in my plastic folder and produced the cab driver's change. I offered him a handful.

'There you are, luv, just the ticket.' He counted out some copper coins as change. 'Foreign are you?'

I nodded. Frankly, I felt pretty foreign at the moment.

'Well Bon Jour, Buenas Dias, Auf Wiedersehen, I'm sure,' he said tipping his cap to me and he continued bawling: 'Stan-ard, Stan-ard, Evenin' News . . .'

At that point there was an ear-splitting sound of revving engines and a stream of motorbikes came roaring up the Kings Road. Well, bikers hadn't changed much anyway. Except that these Hell's Angels looked about twenty years younger than the ones I was accustomed to seeing.

The news vendor had turned to another customer, an old gentleman wearing a black felt hat, and the two of them were having a good old tut-tut together about the shockingly evil tendencies of 'modern youth'.

At that point something else caught my eye. A pavement artist had been working in the Square. I crossed to see what he had been up to. There was a really elaborate version of the Mona Lisa in coloured chalks and some white horses charging through psychedelic waves. The drawings were brilliant. Beside them was a hat with only a few copper coins in it, so I added one for luck. And beside this, something else caught my eye – on a clean paving slab . . . There it was:

LOVE.

Four stark letters followed by a single full stop.

My heart turned over with a bump. Suddenly the sun shone with more enthusiasm, passers-by gained a spring in their step, Sloane Square was no longer plain old Sloane Square – it was a site of enormous significance – Los had been here, and recently too, the chalk looked quite fresh. He might be still around. But *where*?

I cast a searching glance over the Square – praying for a glimpse of a familiar black mac – a head of tousled tie-dyed hair. But search as I might, he was nowhere to be seen.

I sat down on the edge of the fountain and waited.

It was a busy day, people swept past me, heading towards Peter Jones, or away from it and down into the tube station. It was a desolate feeling watching them go by and knowing that out of the hundreds and thousands of faces not one of them would be Franz's or Henry's because *I was in a different time*. And I couldn't go into 'Oriel' – our favourite café – to have a consoling hot chocolate, *because it wasn't there yet*. And I wouldn't be meeting up with Chuck later at 'Henry J. Beans' because that wasn't either, and I couldn't go round to his house or call him up even – because *he hadn't been born yet!*

I was beginning to feel very much alone and rather lost. As time passed I realised Los wasn't going to show up.

'Here one day, gone the next,' a bitter echo of TeXas' voice came back to me.

But where should I go? What should I do? I counted how much money I had left. I had seven large copper pennies and a strange little pale octagonal coin with 3d engraved on it. That wasn't going to last long. I was already feeling hungry. What did a penniless vagrant do in 1967? Sleep on a park bench? Start begging? Drawing on pavements? Even assuming I could still do my really realistic horse's head – the guy with the psychedelic horses complete with bodies, legs and everything, had only been given a few coins. I could quite easily starve to death.

I searched the plastic file for inspiration, inside was the little green cardboard railway ticket. A ticket to Little Walping, my grandmother's Norfolk home. That was it! I'd go to Grampy's. Grampy would still be at 'Trudgings'. She'd lived there all her life, since the beginning of time, practically.

So I used the pennies to buy a tube ticket to Liverpool Street station.

In the Tube a boy about my age *got up and offered me his seat.* I took it, wondering if maybe I was looking pregnant or something.

The people in the train all looked so incredibly respectable. There were none of the standard '90's ripped jeans and dirty sneakers. Men wore neat suits or proper coats or raincoats and they all had the most unbelievably highly polished shoes. I mean, I bet none of them had holes in their socks even. And the women – they all had their hair permed like Grampy, even quite young women – they had this real lamb-dressed-as-mutton look, lumpy tweed suits and handbags with proper handles held stiffly over the arm like Mrs Thatcher and the Queen. No wonder they had a youth revolution on their hands. Geesus, they needed something to shake them up.

People kept giving me odd looks and I suddenly realised that, by their standards, I must look incredibly scruffy. I mean, I was dressed in a perfectly ordinary polo neck and non-descript black jeans. But come to think of it – no one else was dressed all in black like me. All the females were dressed in pastel shades like yucky yellow, nauseous green and puke pink. I sat there feeling like a crow that had gatecrashed a cage full of disapproving budgies all the way to Liverpool Street.

Some time between 1967 and what I innocently used to call 'the present day' someone has spent the odd few millions on giving Liverpool Street station the most incredible 'make-over'. They've ripped the guts out – all the traditional tatty, grotty, sooty stuff has been replaced by steel and glass and marble-effect composite flooring. And there are loads of little brightly lit boutiques with names like 'Tits n Bums' and 'Thanks-a-Bunch' and 'Down-at-Heels'. And in place of the old wood and brass and marble station buffet, there's antiqued chipboard and polystyrene 'O'Ryans Original Irishe Eating House'.

Well, back in 1967 those millions spent on the make-over were just a gleam in the developer's eye. All the good old grotty authentic stuff was back in place. Together with a load of good old grotty authentic-looking people. You could tell at a glance, they were genuine citizens of 1967. Take hats for instance – I mean, practically every man was wearing one – as if they were some sort of uniform of rank. Bowler hats for the pinstripe city workers, a kind of dun-coloured felt thing for the average bloke in a mac, and caps for anyone who didn't fit into the other two categories.

I hovered by W.H. Smiths, such a darling little news-stand with real mahogany roll-down blinds. On the counter there were magazines with reassuring pictures of people who actually gave credibility to all that 'Swinging Sixties' stuff. They wore hipster flares and outrageous make-up and tried to look unembarrassed by the painfully un-cool headlines like 'Fab Gear' and 'Rave Time' and 'How to Get With-It'!

Eventually, a railway worker in a shiny black suit complete with waistcoat, came out and slotted a wooden sign in a post which read: 'All stations to Norwich'. At the sight of him, everyone moved forward in unison, just one polite step.

When the train drew in there was a lot of careful opening of doors and 'After you' on the part of the men. I found a vacant seat and sank thankfully into it.

It was such an adorable train – all so hand-crafted. It had lots of wood and brass and little string shrimping nets to put the luggage in. Beneath these, brass framed posters proclaimed the delights of 'Holidaying in sunny Bournemouth', the wisdom of insuring your home with the 'Man from the Prudential' and that the place to make new friends was 'Butlins'.

My carriage soon filled up. A whistle was blown and the train pulled out.

I sat staring out of the window, wondering if I was doing the right thing. Maybe Los was in Sloane Square right now. Maybe I should have waited longer. I gazed dismally at the passing panorama of soot-blackened bricks, grimy sidings and crumbling embankments. These were interspersed here and there with bright posters for products I had never heard of. There was one for a washing powder called Tide. With the headline: 'Tide's In Dirt's Out' over a brightly smiling housewife hanging out dazzling washing with the kind of satisfaction she'd get lynched for showing these days. Another for 'Camp' Coffee with a picture of a First World War gentleman in a neat khaki uniform complete with spats who seemed stoically resigned to the implications of the product he was representing. One building had a peeling inscription for something called the British Liver Association – faded almost beyond recognition, and there were loads and loads of metal signs advertising a soap called, most unpromisingly, 'Wright's Coal Tar'.

The train continued through an unbelievably grimy outer London and out into the suburbs of what seemed, in these long-lost pre-tumble-dryer days, to be a nation obsessed by washing. Every garden had its straggling line of sagging sheets and wind-inflated underwear.

I must have fallen asleep somewhere near Chelmsford because I woke later with a start to find we were in deep countryside. Cows for whom BSE was still a dim distant threat, stood happily munching their cud in the same timeless way as their children and grandchildren, and countless future bovine generations would munch after them. It all looked so familiar that I wondered for a split second whether I had imagined the whole weird set of events of the past few hours – I was on my way to Grampy's after all. Everything outside looked totally normal.

Then I turned my gaze on the people in the carriage. They all sat there dressed up like characters from an early episode of the Avengers. There was an old gentleman with a curly black fur collar on his coat. A permed lady in a pale blue bouclé tweed suit. A very aristocratic looking old lady wearing a Queen Mum hat with a turned back brim. And a man who looked like a cartoon spy, in a hat and raincoat with his collar turned up. At any moment you could imagine the train drawing to a halt and Steed's bowler hat appearing through the doorway, and him tipping it back with his umbrella and saying, 'Nobody move. Miss Peel, I have cause to believe we have an imposter in our midst.'

The train stopped for quite some time at Colchester Station. I sat sleepily gazing out of the window watching a pigeon half-heartedly preening itself on a massive sign saying: C O L C H and then as we pulled out of the station, I caught sight of it again on the wall, underneath E S T E R. The word: LOVE.

It was written just like the one in Sloane Square, in fresh white chalk.

My heart missed another dozen beats. This was so-oo weird. Los was somewhere around, but *where*? What the hell could he be doing in Essex of all places? Essex!

I had to get off the train. But – panic attack – there was no handle on the door! The train was moving faster and faster.

'Hold on, young lady,' said the spy gentleman. 'Too late to get off now. You've missed your stop.'

I sank back in my seat and several people in the carriage

made helpful suggestions about getting out and taking a train back at the next station etc and various other sympathetic noises.

While I was recovering from all this attention, a waiter came striding down the corridor in a neat white jacket. He tapped on each carriage door in turn, saying, 'Luncheon. First sitting. Take your seats please in the dining car.'

The aristocratic lady got to her feet and made her way off down the train.

My stomach rumbled, I was now seriously ravenous. Still, I'd soon be sitting down to a meal at Grampy's. It was at that point that I started to have some rather disconcerting thoughts about how I was actually going to introduce myself.

'Hello, you don't know me, but I know you.' 'Surprise surprise! Guess who I am? Actually I'm your future granddaughter.' Etc etc.

The rest of the journey was spent agonizing over finding a way round this problem. By the time we arrived, I hadn't come up with a single workable solution.

The train drew slowly to a stop at Little Walping station, the spy gentleman got to his feet and let the window down by a funny leather strap that looked like a belt and opened the door for me. It seemed that in 1967, train doorhandles were most inconveniently positioned on the outside. I climbed thankfully out and landed safely a long way down below on the platform.

A whistle blew and the train drew out leaving me standing there a lone figure on a long empty expanse of concrete.

'Tickets please . . .'

The ticket collector was leaning over the barrier waiting for me.

I handed him my ticket and found on the other side of the barrier that I had been right about Little Walping. It was about the most backward backwater in the universe. Over the next thirty years the relentless tide of progress was going to make absolutely no impression on it whatsoever. The village was just as I had last seen it.

I made my way thoughtfully down the main street. What on earth *was* I going to say to Grampy? What had seemed such a good idea in Sloane Square, now appeared in its true light – an act of total insanity.

I paused in front of the Post Office, trying to gain inspiration. The little cork notice board with its drawing pinned notices advertising 'Kittens for good homes' and requests for 'Bric-a-brac for Jumble Sales' and entries for 'Parish Flower Shows' was in place as ever. And then another notice caught my eye. It read:

Trudgings
East Lane, Little Walping.
DOMESTIC HELP URGENTLY REQUIRED
Live in or Daily. Excellent remuneration.
References essential.
Apply to: Mrs Morton Telephone: LWL 237

Well, what do you know?

I continued on my way down the road with a lighter step. I soon passed the church with its creaking lych-gate. The same starlings were still carrying on their noisy competitive chatter in the elms, or at least their great great grandparents were. East Lane was as pot-holed and puddled as it had ever been and a deep foam of cow-parsley still clogged the ditches.

And there was 'Trudgings', unchanged apart from a certain green youthfulness in the apple trees that dotted the lawn. And hang on – the old tree stump wasn't a stump any more, it was an ageing oak tree that groaned in the breeze.

I crunched up the drive and pulled on the bell pull. And,

in case you're wondering, I had by now worked out a decent strategy of how to address Grampy.

The door opened and the surprising apparition of a much younger Grampy appeared in the doorway. Her nice soft grey hair had been replaced by a crisp brown head of permed curls. Her whole face looked as if she'd had the most incredibly successful face-lift, it was pink and plump and shiny and slightly fierce:

'Can I help you?' she asked.

For a moment I was speechless. My lovely cuddly, eiderdown-soft, baby-skinned Grampy had been replaced by this aggressively-corseted stranger.

'Mrs Mo-orton?' I droned in a fair imitation of a Swedish accent.

(Why Swedish? Well, Swedish happens to be about the only accent I can do credibly. Jemima, my sister, and I had had this au pair called Olga. Olga had been very, very Swedish. She had big round surprised eyes and this deep lugubrious voice which went up and down like a rocking horse and made all her statements sound like questions. By the time she had been with us three months we could both take her off perfectly.)

'Yes *ec*tually. Can I help you?'

Even her voice sounded different – instead of Grampy's nice soft croaky voice, it sounded like a cross between Celia Johnson in *Brief Encounter* and Princess Anne.

'I've come about the jo-ob?'

'*Eugh*,' said Grampy. 'I suppose you didn't th*e*nk of ringing first?'

'I have a little pro-blem. Please could I speak with you?' I said, doing my best to look tearful.

'*Eugh*,' said Grampy. 'Well, I th*e*nk you h*e*d better come inside then.'

The thing about Grampy is that she might currently *look* fierce on the outside but underneath I knew she was really such a softy. Over the years she's had the most ghastly people working for her because she's been taken in time after time. She just can't help falling for bad luck stories.

So when she heard my terrible tale of the appalling family I'd escaped from in London. How they'd kept me in an icy unheated attic room and made me work non-stop round-the-clock on a diet of cold porridge and tapwater. And what had happened the night I had been left alone in the house with the father of the family . . .

'Say no more . . .' she said patting my hand and pouring me another cup of tea. 'There is *e*bsolutely no question of you going back there. Poor child! What you h*e*ve been through. Which reminds me, by the way, I feel I should ask. How old are you, ex*e*ctly, Helga?'

'Eighteen?' I reckoned if I wanted the job it would be wisest to add on a couple of years.

'Poor dear child. When I tell my husband . . . he'll . . .'

'No please . . .'

Her husband! Of course Grandad must still be alive. I remembered him *just*. A distant genial figure hazily glimpsed through the mists of time or was it the billowing smoke of his perpetual bonfires?

'I understand,' she said, patting my hand again. 'We'll say no more about it. Best forgotten.'

No more was said. I was employed. The question of references wasn't even raised. Actually, apart from sympathising with my plight, Grampy was pretty desperate. She had Aunt Hannah's twenty-first birthday party coming up, and it seemed that, with most unfortunate timing, Mrs Weatherall, her stalwart cook/housekeeper had been rushed off to hospital suffering from appendicitis (with complications).

'Far too late to put the party off. All the invitations R.S.V.P.'d. And the marquee – and the tables and chairs – all due to arrive on the day after tomorrow . . . We'll simply have to make the best of it,' she rambled on as she showed me around the house.

'Hannah!' she called out of the window.

'I'd like to introduce you to my elder daughter,' she said over her shoulder to me. Then muttered to herself, 'Where's she disappeared to this time?'

Hannah! Aunt Hannah! Wild Aunt Hannah – the long-lost, cat-collector who'd almost been erased from our family tree.

'Would you like me to find her for you, Mrs Mo-orton?'

'Oh would you? How kind. I think if you tried the orchard . . . it's down that path, can you see where it goes, over there . . . ?'

She gave me detailed instructions on how to get through a garden I knew probably better than she did. Jemima and I had spent nearly all our summers at 'Trudgings'. Long, damp, dull English summers of incessant squabbling and intermittent rain.

I made my way past the garden shed, now miraculously upright and intact and smelling richly of fresh creosote. Past the cedar tree with the big low branch which was to have a swing added some twenty or so years from now. Through the garden gate which wasn't yet hanging on one hinge because Jemima and I hadn't yet broken it with our combined weight – and into the orchard.

The grass was tall and dense between the apple trees. I swished through it looking for signs of Hannah. I had never met this mysterious aunt. Mummy always referred to her in the past tense and called her 'Poor Hannah'. Last heard of she was researching a book on her favourite subject: 'Catford to Katmandu . . . Ramblings of a feline fancier.'

Anyway, she wasn't doing anything half so active at the moment. A glimpse of fine grey smoke winding up into a gnarled pear tree led me to where she lay stretched out on a big fluffy afghan coat gazing up into the branches.

'Hi,' she said through half closed eyes. 'Who are you?'

'I am your mother's new au pair Miss Mo-orton?' I said, trying to sound authentic.

'Poor you,' she said. 'Call me Hannah. You foreign?'

'I come from Swe-den?'

'Groovy,' she said raising herself on one elbow. She offered her hand-roll. 'Want a puff?'

I shook my head. 'Your mo-other sends me to find you?'

Hannah lay back on her coat. 'Tell her I'll be along soon, OK?'

This mission not accomplished, I returned to the house.

Grampy was waiting for me with an armful of bedding.

'She says she comes in a minute?'

Grampy shook her head and made tutting noises.

'Come along then. We'll get you settled and then I must go to the station to pick up my other daughter, Caroline. I think you'll like her. I bet you two'll have masses in common.'

Caroline! Mummy! Well she was certainly right there. There were half my genes for a start. Mummy in 1967. Which made her . . . Hang on . . . Sixteen! Exactly the same age as me. This was going to be *interesting*.

10

Grampy took me to the station to meet Caroline. She said she wanted to point out the shops in the village.

'And that's Winsome's the Bakers. If you get the boy serving you, remember you have to count the change very carefully. And Bragg the Butcher, always watch while he's trimming the chops, otherwise you'll get all fat . . .'

. . . and there's Plodd the Policeman I added mentally, as the village Bobby went by on his creaking bike. I was starting to feel as if I'd landed in a dramatically challenged episode of *Noddy*.

We came to a halt outside the station just as the train was drawing in.

'I do hope Caroline hasn't missed it this time,' Grampy murmured as we waited at the barrier.

In a strange way I was starting to feel nervous. As if Mummy might be able to see right through my new persona – in that infuriating way mothers have of always knowing what you're up to. Kind of maternal second-sight or something.

I anxiously scanned the platform. As the dense crowd of city suits and sensible coats thinned out, a strange apparition was revealed. Dressed in a white PVC mini skirt and black and white Op Art zip jacket – also in PVC, white tights, black patent shoes, dark glasses and white lips, and freak-out, the, whole lot topped by a lop-sided two-tone butcher's boy cap – it couldn't be!

I wasn't prepared for this. You expect mothers to wear reasonable clothes, or at least unnoticeable ones. I mean, I always thought Mummy had been born middle-aged – the whole purpose of her existence destined to culminate in worrying about me and my life. Mothers were never meant to dress up and put themselves about like this. I mean, basically she looked as if she had a life of her own.

But it was Caroline. She was now kissing Grampy on the cheek.

'Hello Mummy,' she said.

'Hello darling. Had a good journey? You do look a bit peaky. Oh and by the way – this is Helga.'

'Hel-lo?' I said.

'She's Swedish. She's heaven-sent. Going to be our new au pair, aren't you dear?'

'Gosh, I say, that's handy,' said Caroline – giving me a searching look as she unloaded her carrier bags on to me. (It was Mummy's face all right. An earlier model of course – pre-eye-bags and greying-hair – God I hope time isn't going to wreak havoc on my face like it has on hers.)

'Isn't she a bit young?' I heard her whisper under her breath to Grampy as they headed back to the car. I followed with the slippery armful of carrier bags, catching snatches of Grampy's reply:

'. . . nowhere to go poor child . . . awful time . . . tell you later . . . just couldn't turn her away.'

Caroline turned her gaze on me with a 'not-another-of-Mummy's-deserving-causes' look on her face. Grampy held a warning finger to her lips.

I settled in the back of the car with the parcels.

Caroline took off her dark glasses and revealed dense false lashes, one of which was coming slightly askew giving her a drunken lop-sided look.

'Where's she sleeping?' she asked as if I were a dog or something.

'We'll have to clear out the box room,' said Grampy.

'But I've got all my gear in there.'

'Well, we'll just have to re-arrange things a bit, won't we?'

Caroline gave me a hostile look.

'How long is she staying?' she hissed.

'Perhaps we should talk about this later, dear. Did you manage to find something to wear for the party?'

'Gosh yes. I should say so.'

'Well, I hope you got something *suitable*.'

Caroline cast a loving glance over the bags in the back. There was one from Biba. Another that had a sort of target on it with 'Take Six' in the middle. And a third with a stoned-looking female with psychedelic stripes running through her hair and 'Carnaby Gear' scrawled across it.

She hauled an Edna Everage-style lilac feather boa out from the Biba one. 'Look at this. Isn't it gorgeous?'

Grampy was unimpressed: 'We used to wear those in the Thirties,' she said.

In fact, Grampy was unimpressed by most of Caroline's shopping. She held up the 'dress' itself which consisted of a small amount of bias-cut lilac nylon suspended from a T-strap.

'Looks like underwear,' said Grampy examining the hem which was already fraying and coming adrift in places. 'You can't possibly wear this on Saturday.'

'But it's really with-it. Everyone's wearing fab gear like this . . .' objected Caroline.

'Where, who? I haven't seen them,' said Grampy.

'Oh yes, Mrs Mo-orton, I have seen them. In London,' I said helpfully.

Caroline cast a grateful glance in my direction.

'Well, I don't know I'm sure. I'll have to consult your father about it.'

The discussion was adjourned until after supper. Supper! You'll remember I hadn't had any lunch.

'Just a light meal,' said Grampy as I was put to work peeling potatoes. In the subsequent hour, I was taught how to make something called 'Toad in the Hole', a dish which was almost as disgusting as its name suggested. By modern standards of nutrition this particularly noxious recipe would have to carry a Health Warning. Anyway, it's a ghastly combination of sausage and yorkshire pudding which takes forever to prepare.

The meal of lumpy mashed potato, greens and 'under-cooked saturated pork fat in a high cholesterol batter' was served at six o'clock sharp.

I emerged from the kitchen to find Caroline half-heartedly slamming knives and forks down on the table. I caught the tail-end of her conversation with Grampy:

'. . . don't see why she should expect to eat with us.'

'Shhh,' warned Grampy as I approached.

The table was set for five. It appeared that Grampy's modern liberal ideas gleaned from *Woman's Home Journal*, included the fact that an au pair had to be treated as part of the family. I was expected to live like them, enjoy family conversation and to eat like them. Big deal.

'Re-ally Mrs Mo-orton, I would be happy just to have a yo-ghurt in the kitchen?'

'A what dear?'

'A yo-ghurt?'

'What's that dear?'

Hannah enlightened her.

'It's made of soured milk. They eat it all the time in London. It's meant to be really good for you.'

'Really?' said Grampy and she shuddered. 'I'm afraid we don't have any of that kind of thing here, Helga. This is England. We could make you a junket tomorrow, maybe. With hundreds and thousands on it.'

'And by the way,' added Hannah, 'if you're eating dead animal flesh tonight, I'll just have bread and cheese, thank you, upstairs.'

'She's suddenly gone all vegetarian, I'm afraid,' Grampy confided in me, as if it was some kind of disease or something. Frankly, I wished I'd thought of that excuse.

That night I had my first taste of 1960's cuisine. I soon became confirmed in the view that, as food goes, 1967 was the all-time low-point of cookery. The main ingredient of meals seemed to be left-over meat. There were rissoles, which had the addition of extra gristle, and faggots which were wrapped in an unmentionable skin, and cottage pie which was topped with recycled leftover mash.

After these came 'Pudding', good substantial fare, designed to fly straight to the thighs, rich in things like suet and syrup and margarine. Even their names were fattening, things like 'Roly Poly', or 'Suet Sponge' and most obnoxious of all – a white flaccid boiled object with currants in it, called 'Spotted Dick'.

The Colonel – Grandad – loved all of them. His moustache bristled at the sight of good solid British food. He had no time for Caroline who poked at her meal with a fork and hid her fat and gristle under a cabbage leaf.

''Spose you're on some confounded diet or something,' he barked. 'Too much reading women's magazines, gives women ideas. Want to look like a garden rake? Blasted Twiggy woman. You'll never catch yourself a fellow like that.'

'No Daddy,' said Caroline, eyeing her plate.

'It's all just a fad, you know,' he said. 'Passing craze, living on wretched crispbread and lettuce.'

(He was so-oo wrong, of course.)

'Have some Roly Poly, Caroline. Lost your appetite or what? In love or something?'

I kept a tactful silence as I cleared the plates.

Grampy raised an eyebrow. '"It" is coming round this evening.'

Grandad made a 'grrumphing' sort of noise through his moustache and threw his napkin down on the table.

'Huh!' he said. 'Get that young fellow to mow the lawn for me. He can make himself useful for once. All that poncing around in sports cars. Bring back National Service, that's what I say – sort the young fellows out.'

'Honestly Daddy, please,' objected Caroline.

At that point, I heard the distant farty noise of a sports car approaching. It screeched round the bend, and then crunched to a halt on the gravel drive outside.

I hurried to the kitchen with the dishes. From there, there was a good view of the driveway. The car was a red MG with the hood down. As I piled the dishes in the sink, I saw a long lanky figure swing over the car door in a debonair fashion.

"It" was dressed in a black sweater with a CND badge pinned prominently on it, hideous flares and patchwork stack-heeled boots. It was a minute or so before I registered that under the full head of plastered down over-length hair, between that sparse fluff that I think was meant to pass for side-burns was – *Daddy*.

Sad case. I realised that he was trying pathetically hard to look 'trendy'. He was the Sixties equivalent of those '90's guys who try to grow beards or sport straggling dreadlocks in the misguided belief that they'll kindle female 'interest'.

But hang on, maybe he had. Caroline had come out to meet him.

'Hello Travers,' she breathed.

'Hello Puddums. I say, I nearly had the most frightful prang coming round the corner.'

'Puddums!' I don't believe it. And Caroline was smirking coyly at him as if he were James Dean or something.

'What's that book you've got there?'

'*Zen and the Art of Motorcycle Maintenance.*'

'Sounds frightfully brainy.'

'Don't you bother your pretty little head with it.'

I couldn't be hearing this. Why didn't she belt him one with her handbag, or something? He was being *really* condescending. And to think how Mummy bosses him around these days!

'Let's go for a drive somewhere,' said Caroline. 'If we hang around here, Daddy'll catch you and rope you into some beastly job in the garden.'

So they climbed into the car and drove off.

After dinner and after I had finished the washing up single-handed (remember these were primitive pre-dishwasher days), I wandered into the sitting room and threw myself down on the chintz-covered sofa. Imagine how I felt. There was my mother unfeelingly tarting herself about, going off in an open-topped sports car with a guy looking as if she had a potential sex-life for godsake. And here was I, a lone lost female, desperately in love, yet abandoned. It was just so *poignant.*

And another thing – this was meant to be the Sixties for godsake. Where was all that 'Sex, Drugs and Bad Behaviour'? As far as I could see all that 'Swinging' stuff was just massive overclaiming. All I had observed so far was so incredibly suffocatingly *cosy*.

There wasn't even anyone around for a decent chat, they all seemed to have disappeared into the garden. Geesus, how I wished I could call up Franz for a long girly gossip. At around this time of night I'd normally be getting the benefit of Franz's recycled, second-hand sexual thrills. I even craved the familiar sound of Henry's voice, with all her irrelevantly rational opinions, telling me to get a grip on myself.

I wondered where Hannah had got to. I could hear the groan and purr of the lawn-mower on the back lawn and the click, click, click of secateurs among the rose bushes.

I searched the room for inspiration. A very tiny immature television with an embryonic bulbous screen stood on a table in a corner. Well, that was better than nothing. I switched it on.

Something seemed to have gone wrong with the colour and I couldn't find the remote control anywhere. Still there was a dial on the front, so I fiddled with that. Between bursts of fizzing static a couple of programmes struggled to get through to me.

Grampy peered through the window.

'What are you doing, Helga?'

'Do you mind if I watch television, Mrs Mo-orton? I've finished the washing up?'

'No dear, go ahead, but don't fiddle with the dial thing, it might blow up.'

'I was only try-ing to get the colour right, Mrs Mo-orton?'

'The colour?' she said looking at me in a puzzled manner. 'Oh you mean the *contrast*?'

That's when it dawned on me that television-wise, 'Trudgings' was in a *pre-colour era.* God the Sixties were technologically primitive. Fancy having to sit here every night watching all your favourite celebs coming up in graded shades of John Major grey.

That TV presented me with a new insight into broadcasting history. Even back in 'the good old days' it was possible to have two uninterrupted hours of wall-to-wall boredom. Up until nine o'clock the most riveting thing on was an interlude showing some goldfish swimming round a bowl. I entertained myself by trying to work out whether they were synchronising their movements to the music or whether their timing was merely co-incidental.

This was followed by the nine o'clock news which was read with the kind of clipped tone and perfect vowels that went out with Brylcreem. There was some breathlessly hallowed reporting on Her Majesty Queen Elizabeth visiting some place that seems to have since disappeared from the face of the globe. And hang on, I could swear the Queen had on exactly the same dress as in 1997 – guess that's the compensation for having absolutely no fashion sense whatsoever – your clothes simply don't date.

It was at that point the phone rang.

I hauled myself off the sofa:

'He-llo, the Mo-orton household. Can I he-elp you?'

'Hi there!'

I didn't believe I was hearing this! It was Los!

'How on earth did you know where to find me?'

'No sweat. CP112. Couldn't miss it.'

'What?'

This was followed by another voice and a demonic laugh.

'*Don't worry your pretty little head about it.*'

'Was that Phil? What the hell's going on?'

'It's me-ee.' It was Phil's voice. 'Hi there, baby.' They were fooling around, the way boys do when they're together. I could have killed them!

'Put Los back on,' I demanded. 'Please!'

'OK. It's me again,' said Los. 'So how come you uploaded? I didn't think you were exactly the surfing type?'

I wasn't going to give him the satisfaction of knowing I'd followed him, so I tried to make out that ending up in the back of beyond, broke, homeless and thirty years in the past, was the kind of thing I generally did for kicks.

'Basically, *I'm* doing a bit of research. Looking up a branch or two of the old family tree as a matter of fact. So what are you doing here?'

'Oh, just bumming around, you know,' he sounded a bit put out by my question. 'That's surfing – the thrill of the thing. You never know where you'll end up.'

And I suddenly had a triumphant little thought – I mean, come to think of it, who precisely was following who?

'But it's a bit of a coincidence isn't it, you *ending up* here?'

'Hey. Well why not? It's a really cool wave. You know the Sixties. Swinging London and all that stuff. "Storming", as you'd say. You must be enjoying yourself.'

'I'm not in London,' I pointed out acidly. 'I'm marooned at my grandmother's. And it's not swinging, it's not even vaguely swaying in the breeze. It's numbingly excruciatingly boring.'

'Like us to come and liven things up a bit for you?'

'How do you mean?'

'They're having a party tomorrow, aren't they? Real slap up do?'

'How did you know?'

'CP141 2 151.' It was Phil again, there was more stifled

laughter. I could hear TeXas killing herself, so TeXas was there too.

That's when I really lost it. 'Geesus! Can you stop using that lame, techno-jargon. It's just not funny that's all!'

I could hear Los telling them both to shut up. And then his voice came on again, warm and reassuring: 'Hey . . . slow down. Cool it, Justine. It's OK. I'm going to come and get you, all right?'

'You are. When?'

'Let's just say we'll meet up IRL. I mean, in the real world. *Real* soon.'

'Where, when, how? Los, listen. You can't just leave me here like this!'

There was a noise that sounded as we were being cut off.

'Don't ring off. You can't! Tell me where you are?'

But it was no use, the phone had gone dead.

'Who was that?' asked Grampy standing in the hall with one gumboot on and one off.

'A wrong number, Mrs Mo-orton.'

Geesus, I might have known it. TeXas was with him. What were they up to? As I returned to the television, I was having some deeply disturbing doubts about Los. How did he really feel about me? Did he feel anything? Maybe he was suffering from that worrying male condition Franz, Henry and I called 'library syndrome'? Why buy a book, when you can basically take out anything you fancy?

Maybe he was going out with TeXas after all. I slumped back on to the sofa, miserable and confused.

In complete and callous contrast to my mood, the newsreader had become quite jovial during my absence. There was some footage of The Beatles arriving to a reassuring scene of mass hysteria at London Airport. Crowds of teenage girls were writhing and screaming and chewing their handkerchiefs. This was more like it.

I went up to bed at around ten – exhausted. A small lumpy put-you-up bed had been found for me in the box room. I lay there for ages unable to sleep, wondering what on earth I had got myself into. There was music coming from Hannah's room, a sort of continuous strumming on a guitar accompanying a kind of angry wail of protest which didn't help much.

Los said he'd be here soon. What was soon? Tomorrow? The day after? Tonight maybe?

At around one in the morning, I heard the sound of the MG coming very slowly to a stop in the lane. There was a very, very long pause and then the crunch of footsteps on gravel told me that Caroline was back home and she wasn't alone. There was another long pause and a scrabbling sound outside in the bushes. And then Caroline's voice in a frantic whisper:

'No, I say, Travers, honestly!' (giggle) 'Shhhh! We'll wake someone.'

Then there was a further, longer pause and more scrabbling noises.

What was going on out there! This was positively pornographic. Honestly, these were my parents. It was *disgusting*! I considered leaning out of the window and telling them to behave themselves.

But then the front door clicked closed and I heard Caroline creeping up the stairs. Daddy's footsteps crunched across the gravel as he made his way back to his car.

Well really! I thought. And then I must have fallen asleep.

11

You can have no idea of the *inconvenience* of living in a pre-technological world.

I was rapidly coming to a conclusion. It wasn't the feminists who had liberated modern woman, it was the engineers. The basic equipment in Grampy's house was positively stone age. She introduced me to this monstrosity known as a 'Twin-Tub'. Call it a washing machine? After washing, everything had to be dragged out of one drum and slopped into another, mangled, hauled out into a basket and pegged out to dry – which took hours. How 1960's woman got the time to get liberated beats me. You'd think she'd be too bloomin' busy.

Pre-duvet bed-making was another challenge. I was initiated into the mysteries of how to make something called 'hospital corners'. You had to fold crisp starched sheets into sharp triangles before you tucked them in. Grampy stood over me until I got it right.

Then I was left to: 'Tidy Caroline's bedroom and dust.'

You won't believe this but I actually found myself *putting all the tops back on her make-up and hanging up her jeans.*

I was well into this humiliating role-reversal when Caroline sidled in.

She was wearing lime-green hipster flares and an orange skinny knit jumper and she had her hair done up in bunches. Bunches! She sat on the chintz-covered window seat and watched me for a while. I could feel myself positively prickling with indignation. She was the one with time on her hands. Why the hell couldn't she tidy her own room, for godsake?

Then she said in an embarrassed sort of voice, 'Helga, could I ask you something?'

'Yes, of co-ourse?'

She got up and went over to the bedroom door and closed it. Then she sat down again, this time on the end of the bed. She leaned forward and said earnestly, 'Is it true what they say about Swedish girls? How you're more kind of *liberated* . . .' she paused.

'About wh-at?'

'Well, you know, all that umm . . . you know, before you get married or maybe before you're engaged even . . . ?'

'Do you mean sex?'

She stared at the floor. 'Yes.'

'Oh ye-es. That is true. We believe in, how you say – free love? In my cou-ntry?'

'Well, what I wanted to ask was . . . I mean last night Travers and I nearly umm. Oh God . . . this is *so* embarrassing . . .'

'I do hope you are ta-king care?' I said.

'That's the thing,' said Caroline looking at me red-faced and damp-eyed. 'I mean the thing is. I'm not too sure how to go about – umm – *taking care*.'

I don't believe I was hearing this. I mean surely they had sex-education in the Sixties? If not, couldn't they get everything they wanted to know out of teen magazines, like we do?

'Don't they tell you all this at scho-ol?'

Caroline shook her head. 'My school's a convent. Reverend Mother says the best form of birth control is abstinence.'

'I see? But what about your mo-other?'

'Oh, I couldn't possibly talk to Mummy about anything like that.'

Actually, come to think of it, I couldn't imagine Grampy mentioning any part of the body more intimate than say 'thigh'. In fact, even 'thigh' was getting pretty heavy for her.

'What about your boy-friend, Travers?'

'I don't think he has the foggiest idea.'

Knowing Daddy, she was probably right.

'So I thought,' continued Caroline, blushing madly. 'Seeing as you're Swedish and everything. You'd be the ideal person to ask . . .'

It struck me at this point that I was in a pretty unique position. I mean how many people do you think have had to give sex-education *to their own mother*.

Oh my God. How did I go about this? I remembered Miss Savage, our Biology teacher in Form One, commonly known as 'Sewage' because of her devotion to brown Courtelle separates, demonstrating the right way to put on a condom using a carrot for a 'prop'. (About the nearest she ever came to the real thing as Franz commented later.) We had all been dead embarrassed, but Henry had helped out by asking intelligent scientific questions about 'third world over-population' and 'fail-safe ratios'.

So anyway, I launched into what I could remember of 'Sewage's' distanced and scientific advice on what she called 'family planning' – which I've always thought meant more or less the opposite.

Caroline listened round-eyed.

'But where do you get er . . . um?' She couldn't quite bring herself to say the word.

'Con-doms? The Che-mist's, of course?'

'That's out of the question, then,' said Caroline. 'Mr Freeman's known me since I was born, practically. He'd be bound to tell Mummy.'

She sat and stared out of the window for a minute, screwing up her handkerchief in her hands. Then she turned to me.

'But he doesn't know you . . . Helga.'

So that's how I happened to be in Little Walping, at Freeman's Family Pharmaceutical and General Store, standing in front of a massed display of aggressive-looking hairbrushes, trying to pluck up courage.

The condoms weren't laid out in a nice friendly display like they were back home in Boots, where people could pick them up and chuck them in their wire basket with the nonchalance of one selecting one's favourite flavour of chewing gum. I realised with a sinking feeling that they must be somewhere behind the counter.

Mr Freeman was looking at me expectantly.

I stalled for time.

'Have you any thro-at pastilles?' I asked.

He had a lot of different kinds of throat pastille and I hoped I was building up some kind of rapport with him as we went through them.

'Will that be all, miss?'

There was a pause that lasted half a lifetime.

'Do you sell con-doms?' I blurted out.

He looked at me as if I'd demanded some illegal substance. I was glad I'd at least taken the precaution of wearing my ring back to front so it looked like a wedding band. I shifted the hand with the ring on it to a more prominent position.

He leaned over the counter and asked in a stage whisper, 'What kind would you like, Mrs er . . .'

I hadn't been prepared for this.

'Well, you see they're not for me . . .' I started, and then realised how ridiculous this sounded. 'I mean . . . any kind. The usual, you know?'

He gave me another very suspicious look and shoved a small package into a white chemist's bag and handed it over the counter.

I left the Chemist's feeling like a criminal, with the packet safely tucked away in my pocket. Geesus – *the things one has to do for one's parents!*

When I arrived back at 'Trudgings', I found that the place was rapidly being transformed into what looked like the venue for a circus. There were miles of rope and piles of massive tent pegs all over the drive. Piled up neatly in the centre of the garden was enough striped canvas to make a couple of big tops.

Vast blokes stripped to the waist were hard at work dashing tent pegs into the lawn. It was starting to look like a battle field. Grandad was in his element, striding round egging them on and warning them to mind an apple tree here and avoid an underground pipe there and generally getting in everyone's way.

'Grand show eh?' he said when he caught sight of me.

I agreed. Grampy appeared in the kitchen window beckoning vigorously.

'Oh Helga, where have you been? They all need tea and the chairs have arrived – and there's absolutely nowhere to put all these glasses – I've no idea where the girls have got to. What we're going to have for lunch I really can't say – what a day!'

She was hemmed in with boxes full of glasses and bottles and beyond her a tangled mass of upturned chairs filled the passage and hallway, making her a prisoner of the kitchen.

'Don't worry, Mrs Mo-orton. I am here to help you.'

So true.

I don't want to go into that day in detail. Suffice to say that by the end of it my hands were red with washing glasses. My back ached from humping boxes of bottles. I had burns all the way up my arms from ironing table cloths and bruises all the way down my shins from carting spikey loads of chairs to the marquee. By mid-morning this had risen majestically from the lawn like a hot air balloon being inflated, to sounds of heaves and groans and puffs and blows and eventually cheers. Now it stood swaying gently in the breeze in all its green-striped splendour.

The one bright spot in the day had been a mercy dash Hannah and I had made in the car to Great Walping to get 'lunch' from Sainsbury's.

I had made sure I was in on this trip. My idea had been to sneak a few decent provisions into the trolley – like Fromage Frais and Coco Pops and Chocolate Mousse. But when we got to Great Walping I couldn't for the life of me see where Sainsbury's was.

'It's somewhere over there, I think,' said Hannah waving me vaguely in the direction of an ominously rustic-looking grocer's shop.

Sure enough it had 'J. Sainsbury' written in grand looking gold letters over the shop window. But inside, nightmare!

There were no gleaming white floors and decently stacked aisles. No chiller cabinets of nice glossy pre-packed food to chuck in the microwave – had there been such things, of course. Just cold white expanses of marble counters with signs offering the choice of produce as: Cheddar, plain or coloured, Bacon, back or streaky and Boiled Ham, carved to customer requirements.

There was a man with a straw boater and a blue-and-white striped apron who stood behind the counter looking at me. Having established who I was, where I came from and how Grampy's leg/dahlias/daughters were, we got down to business.

I waited while slabs of Cheddar were cut with a wire, while bacon was sliced and weighed, while ham was cut medium-to-thin with a carving knife. Meanwhile, I scanned the shelves. What a culinary desert – an arid world of baked beans, custard powder, gravy browning, tinned soup, pickled onions, jelly and blancmange powder. And to think how the older generation rave on about the good old days. What they omit to tell you is that orange juice meant squash, you had to cross the Channel for a decent wedge of Camembert and kiwi fruit hadn't yet made it north of the Equator.

I sat in the car feeling very hungry and depressed on the way back. But I didn't have time to dwell on my misfortune because I was kept well and truly occupied from then on. You wouldn't believe there could be so much fuss about a party. But at last, Grampy had arranged the final flower, I had creased the last snowy damask napkin into a lop-sided fan, and the glasses all stood in gleaming pyramids ready for the guests to arrive.

'Well done Helga, I think that's it,' said Grampy and she bustled off to 'have-a-bath-and-get-half-way-decent'.

I wandered out into the garden. The marquee stood swaying gently on its guy ropes.

Everything was ready. A faint evening breeze ruffled the rhododendrons, wood pigeons fluttered back and forth from the dovecote. A thin wisp of smoke from the orchard told us that one of Grandad's perpetual bonfires was burning itself out. The air smelt of mown grass and woodsmoke. It was a perfect English afternoon – apart from the noise of course . . .

An earsplitting discord of 'Love, love me do . . .' and 'The times they are a-changing . . .' blared out from the two girls' bedroom windows as the Beatles vied with Bob Dylan for a fair share of the local air-waves.

I went back into the house. Caroline was running backwards and forwards between the bathroom and her bedroom carrying pots and tubes of gungy-looking substances. She had on a green face pack and her legs were covered with a particularly smelly kind of cream that was meant to take the hairs off.

'Helga, can you give me a hand?' she asked.

She had seated herself in front of her three-piece mirror plucking her eyebrows. Her hair was pulled in tight at the back with a band of sellotape and two huge kiss-curls were sellotaped to her cheeks.

'Be an angel and put another record on for me?'

I went to the pile of vinyl beside her record player. She must have had every single Beatles record that had ever been released.

Under the cover of 'Please please me', she whispered, 'Did you get them?'

'The con-doms, yes?'

'You're a real brick, Helga.'

'Oh, it was no-thing?' I said. I took this strange expression to be gratitude.

'But I was wondering if I could ask you one more teeny-weeny little favour?'

'Ye-es?' I didn't like the sound of this.

'Well, I've been thinking. If I've got them. It's going to look well, as if, you know . . .'

'It was your i-dea?'

'Exactly.'

'But it was, wasn't it?'

'Ye-es but . . .'

'You'll never have the nerve to men-tion them?' (Thirty years on – nothing changes, does it?)

'Exactly. So I wondered . . . I mean. You couldn't sort of ever so casually slip them in his pocket – when he's not looking. Just in case. Could you? . . . Please Helga . . .'

After all the hassle I'd been through to get them it seemed ludicrous to back down now.

'Oh, all right, I suppose so. I'll try.'

Her expressions of gratitude were interrupted by a wail from Hannah.

Hannah, who had treated her hair with henna and had left a bright orange rim around the wash basin, was dragging the ironing board into her room. She instructed me on how to iron her hair from the parting down to the ends. It responded by coming out sleek and glossy, I would never have believed it.

'Storm-ing,' I said when I saw the finished product.

'Pardon?' Hannah's face was flushed with the effort of bending over.

'I mean, you look co-ol?'

'You do say the strangest things, Helga.'

There was another shout at this point from Caroline's room. I found her with ten wet nails trying to apply a false eyelash.

Fixing a false eyelash on someone else's eye requires the kind of split second timing and manual precision that it takes to dock a space-craft. I reckoned that by the third try I had got one eyelash vaguely into position.

She stared in the mirror with just the beginning of what I have subsequently come to know as 'Mummy's mirror face' then ripped the eyelash off announcing: 'I'll have to do it myself.'

Grampy was calling from her bedroom: 'Hannah. What time did you ask the band to arrive?'

Hannah called back: 'How should I know. It wasn't me who spoke to them.'

'Then it must have been Caroline.'

'Don't ask me. I don't know anything about it,' said Caroline.

'Then who did?' said Grampy. 'And more to the point. Where are they?'

But I wasn't concerned about the band. I was more concerned about a more immediate and pressing problem. What was I going to wear? But it seemed Grampy had thought of that.

My 'outfit' was hanging on a hanger from the picture rail in the box room. It was a black dress with a white apron. A waitress's dress. Surely she couldn't expect me to wear that?

I climbed into it crossly. It was made of horrible black scratchy serge, like a school uniform. It reached to that charisma-killing length just below the knee. But I had nothing else. I tied on the apron. I looked a fright.

Caroline came out of her room. She was wearing the lilac nylon T-strap dress. It reached to approximately half an inch below the knicker line. Her face was blanked out by matt white pan-stick. Her lips were a glossy shade of intensive-care mauve and her eyes were two huge inky pools surrounded by thick layers of spider-leg lashes.

That's when the whole incongruous nature of the situation really got to me. She was my mother for godsake! Mothers aren't meant to dress up for parties. They are meant to stay decently out of the way in the kitchen doing menial things and then make themselves scarce when the party gets nicely out of hand. They can be helpful if there's a police raid or something but basically they're best well out of the way till it's time to mop up the puke and broken bottles and stuff in the morning. I should have been the one all dressed up ready to rave for godsake. Not her.

'How do I look?' she asked flicking her feather boa over her shoulder.

'Very with-it,' I said nobly.

That's when I heard the first strains of music coming from the marquee. The band must have arrived after all. The music floated up through the open windows . . . surely I recognised that tune.

I strained my ears.

There was no mistaking it.

'Can you hear that? They are play-ing that Beatles song, you know "Magical Mystery Tour" . . . Listen . . . ?'

Caroline looked at me blankly.

'Magical what?'

'Magical Mystery Tour,' I repeated.

Hannah had emerged from her room. You couldn't imagine more of a clash of styles. She had on a gothic gown of purple velvet that reached to the ground, her hands, which finished in a bunch of black-enamelled nails emerged from medieval sleeves lined with cerise satin. Her lips were painted a deep shade of prune.

'What's a "Magical Mystery Tour"?' she asked.

'The Beatles number?'

They both stared at me as if I were mad. 'What Beatles number?'

A gust of breeze carried the music in through the window with greater force. It suddenly occurred to me. That was the one record Caroline didn't have . . . could it be . . . *that it hadn't been released yet* . . . ?

12

I ran down the stairs two at a time.

The marquee stood quivering in the centre of the lawn. I peeped through a gap in the canvas. The group had set up their equipment at the far end. There were three figures on the platform. A single shaft of light shone on the figure furthest from me, lighting up *his tousled tie-dyed hair*.

My heart turned over with a thump. God I had almost forgotten how absolutely knee-meltingly gorgeous he was. I was about to head across the marquee and enjoy a 'deeply poignant' reunion. And then I thought, Chryst I haven't even had time to put eye-liner on! Geesus what a fright I must look in this gross black dress. I looked *hideous*. Wasn't it just my luck to find myself at, *a major turning point of my life,* dressed like some walk-on part in a third-rate film.

At that point I was collared by Grampy and directed back to the kitchen. For the present, at least, I was 'staff'.

I wasn't alone. It seemed that Loopy Lucy, Dozy Daisy and Manic Maisie from the village had been rounded up for this event. They were hard at work broadcasting local gossip as I poured out glasses of champagne and loaded them on trays.

'That's her there's job, taking drinks roond,' said Loopy Lucy.

'She woon't understand – she's forrin,' said Dozy Daisy giving me a sidelong look as she breathed hot damp breath on a glass and rubbed it with her sleeve. Manic Maisie demonstrated in sign language how to carry the tray and gave me a shove in the general direction of the guests.

The three of them continued to treat me like a deaf-mute imbecile all night.

My evening got off to a roaring start, actually. For the first hour or so I lurked in a draught outside the marquee with a tray of champagne, just praying that Los wouldn't catch sight of me. The form was, that the guests should start with a sort of inspection-of-the-troops down an ill-assorted row made up of Grampy and Grandad, Caroline and Hannah, then grab a glass and head on into the marquee to 'mingle'. The majority of the early arrivals were of the grey-haired variety, ample bosomed or pot-bellied depending on gender. This first lot were obviously friends of Grampy and Grandad with the odd relative thrown in.

One of them, a large bearded gentleman, wearing an impressive row of medals on his dinner jacket, refused champagne and I was sent for whisky.

Hannah smiled in a vague sort of way as he gave her a smacking great kiss.

'I remember dandling you on my knee, by Jove,' said the whisky drinker. 'Cheers!' and he ambled off.

'Who was that?' demanded Hannah, when he was out of ear-shot.

Nobody seemed to know.

A sound of revving car engines in the lane and a great deal of slamming of car doors and 'Haw-haw-haw-ing' noises announced the arrival of what looked like the entire membership of the local Young Conservatives. After making a lot of incredibly naff and dated approval noises like 'Gosh' and 'I say' and 'Ever so groovy' about Caroline's outfit, they swept off with their champagne and started studying the menus and checking place names on the tables to see whether they were seated in positions that reflected their relative importance.

After them, washed and brushed till shiny and looking incredibly uncomfortable in a new-looking dinner jacket came Travers.

'Gosh Puddums,' he said when he saw the length of Caroline's dress. 'I say.'

Caroline pulled at the hem so that the dress covered another half inch or so.

'You don't think it's too short, do you?'

'Golly no,' said Daddy. 'Not in the least. I say, let's dance.'

And they made for the dance floor where the two of them started to perform a series of sad contortions which I guess were meant to pass for dancing.

For the next part of my evening I was promoted to carrying a bottle round and filling people's glasses.

Whenever Hannah held out her glass, it was empty.

'God, this is a drag,' she said as I topped her glass up for the umpteenth time.

'But this is your party. You should be enjoy-ing yourself, no?'

'None of my friends have arrived yet,' she moaned and she took a packet of Rizla papers out of her evening bag and started to roll herself a hand-roll.

'I don't think you should do that here, Hannah.'

'Oh stop being such a bore Helga, will you?'

Well, I suppose she was only trying to keep her spirits up.

Once she'd lit up, she gazed fixedly at the stage.

'Groovy music,' she said. 'Suave guy too, the singer. He's got style.'

I nodded.

Los looked amazing. He was playing a wild mixed compilation of all the biggest hits from the '70's and '80's. Of course, all these numbers were breaking new ground as far as the guests were concerned. Even the most amazingly dated Abba songs got a round of applause.

'He has, hasn't he?' I agreed. I felt a warm glow of pride. I mean it wasn't every girl in the room who had been tracked down by such a perfect piece of male bodywork.

During the third part of the evening I was taken off bottle duty and promoted to serving at table. I was kept well occupied – serving Prawn Cocktail and Duck à l'Orange with three veg to that number of people is no joke. I was just taking a breather before we moved on to the Black Forest Gateaux when there was a pause in the music and Los tapped on the microphone.

I heard his voice say: 'I'd just like to have your attention, please, while I play a special number for a lovely little lady who *isn't* a million miles away from here.'

My heart missed a beat and then I felt all quivery inside, a feeling that went right down my spine.

And then he played Silver Surfer.

Although I was standing in the dark, in my hideous dress, holding a dish of congealing gravy and chewed duck bones, I felt as if a spotlight had suddenly turned on me. I felt as if I glowed with an inner warmth that shone through all the trivial details of what I was doing, how I was dressed etc. Los's voice was charged with emotion as he sang the word 'Venus' with a slight break in it. He was singing about me.

I wished that that moment could last forever . . .

Particularly in view of what happened next. As the last chords died away I heard Los's voice saying:

'That was for Hannah with congratulations and Happy Birthday from us all. Thank you.'

I stumbled blindly towards the exit, colliding with Daisy or Lucy on the way. Somehow I found my way out of the marquee.

'Where you orf to?' demanded Manic Maisie slopping a serving dish in my direction.

I didn't listen. I had been humiliated enough. I dashed upstairs and headed for Caroline's wardrobe. There was no way a female could maintain her self-respect dressed like this. I had to speak to Los, but first I had to find something charismatic and sophisticated to change into – there was no time to be lost.

But this was Caroline's wardrobe. I hauled out and rejected: a psychedelic print nylon mini-dress, a shocking pink crochet hipster trouser suit, a shiny black PVC mini-skirt – interesting – but no top to go with it. Curses! . . . Wait! Hang on . . . What was this? A silver lurex Biba sheath dress had fallen off its hanger and was lying on the floor.

I slid into it. It fitted! It looked pretty good actually although I say it myself. Now for tights . . . The only intact pair had white daisies all the way up the legs – Nightmare! Still this was no time to be choosy. And shoes – thank God for genetics – Caroline and I had exactly the same size feet. I slid on a pair of lime-green patent sling-backs. Lime-green!

Make-up! I did a quick-change-artist's make-over. Blank white face, loads and loads of totally OTT eye make-up. No false eyelashes! I drew little spider legs all around my eyes with eye pencil. A touch of corpse-white lipstick and finally a pair of massive white plastic hoop earrings. Hair! I scraped it all back with a big white alice band. Anyway . . . Here goes!

As I was leaving the room I caught sight of myself in the full length mirror and did a double take. Even *I* didn't recognise myself.

As I returned to the marquee I heard Hannah's voice. To the accompaniment of her guitar, she was droning into the microphone:

'It takes a worried man to sing a worried song . . .' A most unjoyful tune at the best of times, so I guessed her friends still hadn't turned up.

I hovered for a minute outside the marquee, taking a deep breath and pausing just long enough to think of something really memorable to say as an opening line. The time had come to 'Make my entrance' and create a lasting impression of my wit, charisma, and general irresistibility.

'Hel-lo,' said a voice, with that unmistakable undertone of a male who thinks he's on-to-a-good-thing.

It was Travers.

'Hel-lo,' I said rather coldly. He obviously hadn't recognised me. 'It is me. Hel-ga. You know – the au pair?'

'So it is,' said Travers, leaning one arm up against the marquee in what was obviously meant to be a seductive manner. The canvas gave way and Travers almost fell over. Typical!

That's when I remembered the condoms.

Nightmare! Caroline would never forgive me if I forgot. And think of the possible consequences! One elder sister was more than enough!

'Wait there. Got to get something. Don't move. I'll be back,' I said.

Travers obviously took this as encouragement. He gave me a broad wink.

I was shocked. Honestly! . . . Men!

I shot up the stairs as fast as the sling-backs would allow, located the packet in my jeans pocket and clack-clacked down again.

Now all I had to do was to find some way of getting close enough to him to slip them in his pocket, but not too close.

'You like to dance, yes?' I said.

'Rather,' said Travers. 'But let's not go inside. Too crowded.' And he started to slow dance into the rhododendrons. This was just so gross!

'Caroline is a very nice girl, I think,' I said.

'And so is Helga,' said Travers his eyes blissfully closed. He hummed to himself. I think he must have been a little drunk.

I took this opportunity to slip the pack in his pocket.

'That was a very nice dance, thank you, Travers – and now I think we go in-side and join the par-ty?'

'Not yet, Helga. Nice out here. Here, let's have a cigarette,' he patted his pocket and brought out what he obviously took to be a book of matches.

'I say, Helga,' he said, suddenly putting two and two together. 'Gosh . . . I don't know what to say. You Swedish girls . . . I say . . .'

By this time I was making a dash for the marquee. Travers stumbled after me tripping over guy ropes as he did so.

'Helga . . . Wait. I say, Helga.'

We came face to face with Caroline. Her eyes were blazing.

'Yes Travers?'

Inside the marquee someone was banging a fist on the table for silence. A voice was heard to say:

'As godfather, I think I may be *emboldened* to say a few words . . .'

In the lull that followed the whisky gentleman had risen unsteadily to his feet.

'It is so good to see so many . . .' He cast an unfocused gaze over the sea of unfamiliar faces, '. . . so many of *Us* . . . *Here* . . . *On such an occasion* . . .' He swayed: '*Together!*'

The group must be having a break. They had left the stage, they must be outside. I shot back through the exit. Travers and Caroline had disappeared into the rhododendrons and I could hear him attempting to calm her down.

That's when an arm crept around my waist and a voice said:

'As they say in the Movies "I've come to take you away from all this".'

It was Los.

I swung round. 'How could you?' I said.

'How could I what?'

'Sing *my* song for Hannah.'

'*Your* song?'

'"Silver Surfer".'

'She was sitting there all alone. Looking so miserable. I had to do something to cheer her up. It's her birthday.'

'But "Silver Surfer". That's *my* song.'

'*Your* song?'

'Well I just kind of assumed, since you wanted me to be Venus and everything . . .'

'Are we really arguing about a song?'

'Well yes, no, I mean. What do you think?'

'People can't *own* songs. Why do you have to want to own things? Like songs, or, or people for that matter.'

'That is *such* an arrogant thing to say.'

'But that is what the problem is. Isn't it?'

I could feel tears coming into my eyes.

'You don't understand.'

'No *you* don't understand. Can't you see. Things are different where I come from. People don't want to own songs. People don't want to *own* each other.' There was a tortured note in his voice.

'Then why don't you go back there. Go back where you belong. And stay there!' I stormed.

'OK.' said Los. 'If you feel like that. OK, I will. I'll do just that.'

He backed away and then he turned and strode through the tables towards the stage.

I followed him inside. I was hardly conscious of my surroundings, it all seemed a terrible blurr.

The Whisky Drinker was still holding forth:

'. . . to drink a toast to the coming of age of . . . er . . .' His glass tipped dangerously as his mind groped in vain for Hannah's name.

'. . . and what a lovely young woman . . . er . . . *she* . . . has grown up to be . . .'

All eyes turned on Hannah and she smiled in a glazed kind of way. I looked on numbly as he continued, 'It seems only yesterday that I was *dangling* her on my knee by Jove. And then there was school of course . . . where she excelled in . . . but who needs qualifications . . . when you have charm and popularity and . . .'

'. . . and a guy to-die-for dedicating songs to you . . .' I fumed.

'So please will you all be *outstanding* and raise your glasses to the coming of age of . . . of . . .'

He swayed.

Hannah took a deep puff on her cigarette and eyed him defiantly.

'*Heather.*'

The toast was practically drowned out by the roar of

motorcycle engines revving down the lane. Through the gap in the canvas I vaguely registered that a group of long-haired bikers were roaring up the drive. They came to a halt on the lawn. There must have been at least fifty of them. There was minor panic in the marquee as people rose from their tables and the women were hustled to the back. A couple of the Young Conservatives took their jackets off and tried to look fierce. Someone suggested ringing for the police.

'That won't be necessary,' said Hannah.

It seemed her friends had, at last, arrived.

Grampy rose to the occasion and came forward like royalty to be introduced to the late arrivals.

'Nice tent you've got here,' I heard the biggest biker say as he offered a greasy paw. He had long red hair and a flowing beard and was wearing a necklace of flowers and beads around his neck.

'So glad you could come,' said Grampy, trying to look as if she entertained bearded and garlanded bikers every day of her life.

After this, with total disregard for my personal misery, the party cheered up no end. The new guests seemed to encourage people to well and truly lose their inhibitions. Most had given up glasses and were drinking out of bottles. A small group had taken to dancing precariously on the tables. Underneath them people were lying around in a loose group of assorted sexes having a kind of subdued orgy. Roll-ups etc were being passed round. One of the biker boys had decided to do an impromptu strip. A few other lost-looking individuals were wandering about semi-clad. By 1997 standards, it was a pretty average party. By 1967 standards, it was outrageous.

I felt it was a matter of pride to look as if I was enjoying myself, so along with everyone else I hit the dancefloor. I got quite caught up in it all actually. Someone had given me a swig out of their bottle of champagne and someone else had given me a drag of their fag and in general I was starting to feel that the party was going with a swing. I was dancing in an abandoned fashion with practically everybody. I hoped Los could see how popular I was. I made a point of making sure I was in full view of the stage, and with dignity, I studiously avoided catching his eye.

But it wasn't just dancing that was going on. A load of Hannah's friends were having a heated discussion about Banning the Bomb with the Young Conservatives. The biggest and heaviest of the bikers had climbed on top of a table and was saying something about 'fascists' and 'warmongers'.

Grampy and the Whisky Gentleman were taking off their jackets and someone else said something about 'Commies' and 'Reds'. A group of Young Conservatives were building a kind of improvised Berlin Wall out of tables and chairs. And just as this cold war looked as if it was going to turn into a minor holocaust – PC Plodd and most of the local police force arrived on the scene.

There was a sudden hush. Actually, in the uproar I had barely noticed that the music wasn't playing any more.

Hang on, the group wasn't on stage any longer. Where were they? And where was Hannah?

13

'Where's Hannah?' I demanded as I staggered outside.

The big red-bearded biker who happened to be lurking in the shadows outside the marquee cradling a champagne bottle in his arms said:

'Oh, she's split. Gone off with some cool dude musicians, up to London. That's if their van can make it.'

'With who!'

'Those weirdos playing that weirdo music.'

'When . . . When did they leave?' I asked helplessly.

I charged round the marquee to the driveway. He was right. The van had gone. They'd left me behind.

They couldn't have. I ran out through the gates and dodged between cars which were leaving the lane in droves. But the van was nowhere to be seen. They had deserted me . . .

And then suddenly I saw the full horrific significance of it all. I had no idea where they'd gone. I was stranded. Marooned. I could be stuck forever in 1967. OMG!

Grampy was calling me from the kitchen. The guests had nearly all left. The last of the bikers were driving off with ear-splitting revs up the lane. One last peep inside the marquee – which had an aftermath-of-a-nuclear-holocaust look to it – confirmed my view. I had to get out of here fast, no matter how.

'Hey,' I said to the red-bearded biker who was sorting out his crash helmet and climbing on to his bike, 'where are you going?'

'Catford.'

'Catford?'

'We're starting this commune. Big old house. Great big garden so we can grow all our own stuff. Hey sister, we need more girls, why don't you join us? We've got a goat and everything.'

A goat! Boy! Beat that for an incentive?

'Is Catford anywhere near London?'

'Catford's *in* London.'

'Take me with you, then?'

'Climb on behind me, doll.'

So I did.

He thrust down the throttle of the bike and it spluttered into life and then died.

In the stillness before he revved again, I heard Grampy's voice. She was searching through the shrubbery, calling: 'Caroline, Travers. Come out of there. I know you're in there. Come out at once.'

There was going to be all hell let loose in the morning.

The country roads were deserted. I reckon my red-bearded biker must have got his thrills out of speed, I mean the kph kind. Anyway we were going at one hell of a lick and in spite of being scared to death, I was relieved to feel that with each kilometre we were getting nearer and nearer London. I hung on to his massive bulk for dear life, closing my eyes at every corner, which he took at angles I would never have thought possible.

We were just heading towards Chelmsford and had rounded a particularly acute bend in the road when he suddenly slowed down.

'Why are we stopping?' I shouted in his ear.

He nodded towards the side of the road.

There, in a lay-by, standing side by side, propped at odd angles, were a load of bikes and above them, stretched out on a hillock which sloped down to the roadside, were the lumpy forms of sleeping bodies.

Hannah's friends lay in a heap 'doing their own thing man' sleeping off the effects of the party. At the sound of our bike screeching to a halt, a couple of heads were raised.

'Hey man. It's Reddo with that babe from the weirdscene party back there.'

'Hey brother . . . Hey sister. Come'n join us.'

Before I could object we were sharing 'breakfast' in the shape of a round of lagers with them. Someone had started strumming idly a guitar. One of the girls came over and sang a song that was made up of a load of questions which always ended with the most unsatisfactory reply that the answer was 'blowin' in the wind'. It was the most agonisingly frustrating music. Just as I was trying to rev them all into action to move on, the music was kind of slowing them down again.

Eventually, one of the other bikers roused himself enough to prop his head up on one elbow and said to my biker:

'Thought we might mosey up to London and check out the scene, man.'

'Where'bouts?' asked my biker.

It seemed there was going to be this 'Love-in' in Hyde Park. The 'Love-in' was being held to celebrate the fact that the Stones had been acquitted from some drugs charge. And that's where all these guys were heading – eventually.

'So why don't you come with us?' he said. 'It's all for

free. But we gotta get there early if we want to be where the action is.'

'Great, what are we waiting for?' I said encouragingly.

Nobody reacted. They lay around until the sun was well up in the sky. And I was forced to sit there too, seething with impatience. And then just as I was about to give up and start hitching a lift on my own, someone said they thought we ought to make a move.

And someone else said that sounded like a good idea. And a lot of people agreed. And nothing else happened for a while.

And then, one of the bikers climbed to his feet and stretched and brushed himself down and climbed stiffly on to his bike. And then, without a word being exchanged all the others followed his example and I climbed on behind Reddo and we all headed off up the road towards London.

When, at last, we reached London, the bikers roared through the narrow streets attracting maximum attention. We were soon in the thick of youth-culture. The streets were flanked by rows of boutiques which had names like 'Granny Takes A Trip' and 'Psychedelia' and everyone was wearing badges with things like 'Slip it to Me' and 'F.U.' on them. We kept being stopped by hooting traffic jams and getting caught up in one-way systems. And then all of a sudden, we were in Carnaby Street – mecca of the Sixties.

Boy! – even the pavement was painted red white and blue!

As far as the eye could see, Union Jack colours fought with psychedelic swirls of day-glo. This is where Mondrian, met Victoriana, met Op Art, met Art Nouveau with a brave dash of Pop Art slipped in for luck – it was a wild mish-mash of clashing cultures. From each doorway the Beatles battled with the Stones, fighting with the Animals to see who could pump up the volume the highest. Basically, biking down the street was like being trapped in a giant kaleidoscope that was being shaken by some acid-crazed alien. Swinging! Man, the whole scene was reeling!

After Carnaby Street we swung round Oxford Circus and then roared five abreast up Oxford Street. All along the pavements there were crowds of people who all looked as if they'd come dressed up for a totally OTT 'Come-as-the-Sixties party'. Delicate males with masses of long hair and tiny-weeny, thigh-splitting velvet hipsters were being marched along by big strong girls on endless legs topped with microscopic mini-skirts. And they were all heading in the same direction.

The bikers came to a halt at Speaker's Corner. I climbed off and Reddo lurched the bike on to its prop and someone said:

'So let's get in there and start "loving" man.'

But Reddo shook his head. 'Gotta get back to Catford.' He turned to me. 'Coming with me?'

As a matter of fact, I wasn't too wild about the idea of being 'loved' by a massed rank of unwashed and hairy bikers. But since the choice was either that, or a commune with a goat in Catford, I plumped for the 'Love-in' anyway. So as Reddo set off I followed the other bikers into the Park.

It seemed that the 'Love-in' was pretty popular seeing as it was free and in the open air and the weather was good. So whether they were singles or couples or groups or just hopeful hangers-on who didn't look as if they had a hope in hell of a peck on the cheek, they'd all come to Hyde Park in search of 'Love'.

Once in the Park, you could hardly see the grass for bodies

– and I'm talking about that green growing stuff. As far as the eye could see there were people dressed as if they'd raided their grannies' wardrobes behaving in a very un-grannyish way. There were a load of Stones fans, of course, giving the Love-in their whole-hearted support. I guess it was their way of showing the world that their heroes deserved to get off their drugs charge. But it seemed a pretty odd way to celebrate if you ask me, seeing as most of the people within sight looked as if they were either indulging in, or were about to indulge in, the very thing the Stones had just managed to prove they weren't doing.

Then in the midst of all this highly concentrated flower-power, a familiar figure caught my eye. Actually, she wasn't too difficult to spot. She was in her element. She had taken the long silk scarf from around her head and was waving it to and fro in the air like a football supporter.

'Look, it's Hannah!' I shouted, pointing her out.

'So it is,' said someone else. 'And there are all those cool-dude-cat-musicians with her.'

It was true, right behind her was Phil and beside him was TeXas and beside her, gazing in our direction and shading his eyes from the sun was . . . Los.

I stumbled over people forcing my way over and under and in-between 'lovers'. It felt like running on the spot. But at last I thrust my way through the mass of entangled bodies and reached him.

'Hi there,' said Los, maybe the sun was still in his eyes. At any rate he wouldn't look full at me.

'Hi,' I said.

'Come here,' he said and held out an arm.

I stepped forward, not sure what was going to happen next and said, 'I thought you'd run off with Hannah.'

'Come closer,' he said.

I took another step.

'That's more like it.'

He wrapped his arm around me and then the other arm and gave me a long, slow hug. Then he gave me an even longer, slower kiss. And then he looked full at me with an absolutely irresistible expression. I was caught by the gaze of those blue eyes of his. Boy, looking into them was like drowning in deep, fathomless water.

We were just getting to the really good bit when Hannah interrupted us by presenting Los with a handful of daffodils.

'Why is she giving you flowers?' I demanded.

Los sighed, 'Hannah is giving everyone flowers, in case you hadn't noticed.'

He was right. Hannah had taken her shoes off and was doing a kind of Isadora Duncan act with an armful of flowers she had culled from the Hyde Park flower beds. She was selecting highly favoured people at random and presenting them with flowers, saying: 'Peace brothers and sisters,' and 'Love each other.' It was all terribly toe-curlingly embarrassing and un-cool.

'We're thinking of moving on soon,' said Los.

'Good idea,' I said. Personally, I wasn't too wild about public 'loving-in'. The whole thing smacked too much of those ghastly massed teen snogging sessions – frankly I'd grown out of all that.

'Where were you thinking of going?' I asked.

'Back to 3001,' he said in a matter-of-fact sort of way.

'Did you say 3001?'

'Yep. Back to where we come from.'

'*Three-thousand and one*?

Los nodded. 'I want you to come with us.'

'But that's more than a thousand years away. I mean, even further, coming from here.' There was a note of panic in my voice.

Los put his arms around me.

'But I'll be there,' he said.

I cleared my throat, 'Do you think I could have a moment or two to think about this?'

I sat there at the Love-in like the 'only one at a party to have missed out on the swig from the vodka bottle' having serious terror-vibes. I stared at all the square miles of people intertwined with people. And it suddenly struck me that these weren't just people. They were *young* people – all about the same age as me. Except that they weren't *really* the same age, because once I got back to 1997 they'd all be well past their 'best before' date and I'd still be in my prime. And if I got to 3001, they wouldn't be there at all. And nor would anyone I cared about. Not Franz or Henry or even Chuck. And I suddenly realised I missed them all dreadfully. I even missed my mother and father for godsake. I couldn't just surf off to another millennium. I had my own life to live first.

It made me feel a bit humble, actually. OK, stop the jeering – I'm not coming over all Michael Jackson on you – but it did. I mean, where was all that time going to disappear to?

Los had settled down. He was curled up against me. Hang on – he was asleep. Typical! I watched him as he slept. His eye-lids flickered as some dream passed through. And he smiled to himself. And as he lay there like that, I suddenly saw him for what he really was. Just another boy. He wasn't so different from the general run of males I'd met in my time – just a more extreme case. I mean most guys spend their time hassling and changing their minds and swopping around and flitting from girl to girl, especially if they look like Los. At heart he was a surfer. And just like his beach equivalent, he was just a guy hanging around for the biggest waves and the coolest babes. And that was all I was. Just one of the babes he'd met along the way.

That's when I realised, I'd been wrong about all that stuff about 'growing up' all of a sudden. I hadn't really grown up at all. No way! Who wanted to grow up? That's what all these Sixties people were fighting for. The right to be young. And all I wanted to be was young and sixteen right there where I was meant to be in 1997.

Los woke up at that point. I was just trying to break the news to him that I really didn't think I could throw up everything and surf off into the sunset with him, when my voice was drowned out. There was one hell of a racket coming from the Bayswater Road. It sounded like a riot or something.

Phil climbed to his feet. 'Sounds interesting,' he said.

Being surfers, of course, Los and Phil and TeXas just had to go and have a look-see to find out what was going on.

I tagged along as they forced their way through the tangled 'lovers' and out into the road. It was like some kind of massive procession or demonstration. In fact, come to think of it, it was a demonstration. There was a person coming up behind us with a placard which had: LEGALISE POT written on it.

We ventured just a little way out into the street, trying to get a better view of what was going on. And then, without warning we were caught up in it. Whether we liked it or not, we were being swept along by the crowd. It was really scary.

Los grabbed my hand and said, 'Hold on tight and we'll get out of this.'

We were mixed in with a whole load of people who had other placards which bore messages like: TURN ON, TUNE IN, DROP OUT and others with PEACE AND LOVE written on them.

And there was this guy who had a skull mask on and his body all bound up in bandages and I suddenly had this incredibly strong feeling I'd seen him somewhere before.

He was carrying this placard which read: MAKE LOVE NOT WAR.

I *had* seen him somewhere before. But I couldn't think where.

This guy and a load of angry people shouting slogans were bearing down on us fast. Los tried to pull me out of the way.

I really couldn't think straight because I was being hassled by someone else who was dragging me in the opposite direction. A couple of guys pushed into us roughly and at that moment my hand lost hold of Los's.

I grasped at thin air.

I could see his outstretched hand as we were being wrenched apart by the force of the crowd. But I couldn't reach it. We were millimetres apart. And then the gap widened to metres. And it got wider and wider . . .

There was a terrible racket of whistles and sirens coming from behind me. I swung round and saw a ragged row of policemen in riot gear approaching in a grim, purposeful line. I caught a last fleeting glimpse of Los's face as he was engulfed by the crowd. Then the police stormed through and the crowd split us apart.

Police horses with riot shields over their eyes were easing people back. The crowd had become two separate factions of shouting people.

Apart from me that is. Somehow, I had become caught like some sort of soft and very vulnerable buffer between the Demo and the Police.

One very officious policeman was shouting at me through a loud hailer to get out of the way. Then the guy with the skull and bandages threw his placard into the road and ran for it.

In a kind of reflex action I picked it up. I just stood there frozen to the spot holding it. I didn't know which way to jump. The police came to a halt too for a moment, unsure of what to do next. I stood facing them, with what must have looked to the crowd like defiance.

Then one of the demonstrators shouted 'Bravo'. And everyone in the crowd whistled and cheered and roared applause. At the very same moment a photographer leapt out in front of me and took a picture.

Suddenly I was some kind of hero. People were pulling me back into the crowd to congratulate me. But in the confusion I was being dragged further and further away from where I had last seen Los. There were strangers' arms around me and loads of people trying to shake me by the hand.

I kept on saying, 'I've got to go back. I've lost someone.'

But nobody seemed to listen, or care. They carried me along with them up the street and through to Grosvenor Square. They gathered outside the American Embassy and then all hell let loose. The demonstration was getting ugly, stones were being thrown and the police were charging at the crowd with batons raised. I struggled my way to the back, pushing and shoving until I got through all the people and out into the open. And then I ran, I just ran blindly, until all of a sudden I found I was on my own. I was in a tiny side street and I could hear the roars of the angry crowd echoing back from the Square.

I was alone and scared and it was getting dark. And worst of all I had lost sight of Los *again*.

There was only one place I could think of going where I might find him – Portobello Road.

14

I had to walk for ages to get to Portobello Road. The streets were ominously dark and sinister at that time of night. The only sound came from open pub doors and when I passed there was a stench of beer. At one point a drunk tottered out in front of me.

I was heading down to the far end of the road, to the place where I had seen Los doing dodgy deals with the guy with dreadlocks. Newspapers fluttered in the gutter and the last remnants of vegetables showed me that I was in the right place for the the vegetable market. I searched along the street for the place where the bar called 'Seventh Heaven' had been.

I found a staircase that looked very much like the one I remembered which led up from the street. Inside on the wall was some lettering scratched in chalk. It read:

THos PETERSON
TEMPUS FUGIT TRAVEL Co
All destinations catered for
You name it, man!

WYSIWYG.

Old Tom Peterson! I made my way up the stairs two at a time.

But it wasn't *old* Tom Peterson. It was a much cleaner, younger, less tattered version of my old friend.

'Tom Peterson?'

'The very same.'

'I'm looking for someone. Los?'

'Justine?'

'Yes! Is he here?'

'Came through here earlier. They've all gone on ahead.'

'They can't have. Where to?'

'Back to where they came from. 3001.'

'But they can't have just left me behind?' I guess there was a note of mild hysteria in my voice.

'Hey hey. Don't you fret. They've gone ahead, that's all. We'll get you there in no time.'

'But I don't want to go to 3001.'

'You don't?'

I shook my head.

'So where is it you want to get back to?'

'1997. That's where I belong.'

'Hey – a pre-third-Millennium-babe. From the primitive times, eh?'

Considering we were currently in 1967, I thought that was a bit heavy.

'1997?' He whistled through his teeth. Then he rummaged through a pile of papers and drew out a tattered list: '1999, '98 '97. Yep, here we are. That shouldn't be a problem.'

He started searching through a load of disks that looked like photographic plates. The work benches were littered with bits of cable and electrodes, it all looked terribly amateurish – like something out of a very old and dated episode of *Dr Who*.

At last, he selected the plate he wanted and fed it into a

contraption that looked like a cross between an ultra-modern sculpture and a pile of junk. It had the circuit board from a record player amplifier roughly cobbled to the accordion nozzle of one of those really ancient cameras. There were thousands of wires soldered into a spaghetti junction of connections hanging down behind it.

'Are you sure that thing's reliable?' I asked.

'State of the art, no worries,' said Tom. He whistled to himself as he peered through an eyeglass and made a few last-minute adjustments.

'So what's the number you accessed through?'

'Accessed?'

'Uploaded?'

'Oh that! Yes . . .' Luckily Los's e-mail number was indelibly imprinted on my memory, 'http://www.love@300lad.com.'

He tapped it in and then he told me to sit down under what looked very much like an operating table lamp.

'Ready?' he called. 'Sit very still then. Watch the birdie!'

There was a dazzling flash. When the dazzle cleared I could see that I had travelled *precisely nowhere*. Big deal!

Tom rose to his feet with a sigh.

'Must have a loose connection somewhere,' he said. He sucked through his teeth in a disapproving manner. 'There you go you see. I keep telling them. The Sixties here is about as far back as you can go, man. Real frontier country. Technology as primitive as it comes. Back any further and you'd be trying to harness steam-power to windmills . . .'

He whistled as he ran a screwdriver over the connections.

I stood around and waited.

'Well I've run all the checks – all seems OK to me,' he said scratching his head again. 'Must be some problem the other end.'

I'd had this sinking feeling before. It was the kind

of anguish that only the technologically-challenged truly suffer – a painful cross between aching doubt and blind panic . . .

'The computer. Do . . . you . . . think . . . it matters much if-it's-not-plugged-in?'

'*Not . . . plugged . . . in*?'

'You see, it was making some weird noises, like it was going to explode or implode or something – so . . . I . . . pulled-out-the-plug.'

'You did what?' Tom stared at me as if I'd just confessed I'd mugged a granny or turned cannibal or something.

'Fizzing noises. I was positive it was going to blow up . . .' I ended weakly.

'That's it then,' said Tom, slamming his cap down on the bench.

'Is it serious?' I asked.

'I'll think of something,' said Tom.

'Like what?'

'Like we could kind of hang around till 1997 and then plug it in ourselves,' suggested Tom, lying down on a work bench and pulling his cap down over his eyes. 'We've only got to wait thirty years.'

'Maybe we could get someone else to plug it in,' I suggested.

'Who?'

'Isn't there any way to get in touch?'

'From 1967? With this kind of primal pre-technology. You must be joking,' said Tom.

'Oh . . .' was all I could think of to say. I think I started to cry at this point.

'Don't you worry – old Tom'll take care of you.'

I'm sure it was kindly meant, but at that point, a ghastly vision rose before my eyes, of me and Tom in 1997, with our double supermarket trolley, huddled together for warmth in the sheltered bit outside Chelsea Fire Station.

God, everything was a mess. Why on earth had I trusted life and limb, body and soul, to a load of irresponsible surfers? Chuck had been right. They were not to be trusted.

I slumped down on a chair. If only Chuck were here, he'd know what to do. And that's when I suddenly realised how much Chuck meant to me. He wasn't like any of the other boys I knew. He was always there for me. There was nothing Chuck wouldn't do for me. And we belonged to the same time. And that's where I wanted to be. But at this rate, when I got there, I wouldn't be the current 'me'. I'd be middle-aged. I'd be . . . (I did a lightning calculation). I'd be *forty-six* for godsake! Nightmare!

Tom and I sat around all night feeling really despondent. Every now and again my hopes would be raised – Tom would have an idea and say: 'What if . . . ?' And I'd feel hopeful. And then he'd think of some technical reason why it wouldn't work and we'd both slump back into despondency.

I must have fallen asleep just before dawn because I woke to find Tom shaking me by the shoulder.

'Wake up,' he shouted. 'It's come right. I don't know how. But it's working again!'

My eyes focused on the ancient operating table lamp above me as it flashed into life.

'Hey. That's it,' was the last thing I heard.

15

It was Chuck who filled me in on how I actually got back.

It seems he had arrived home from a late night showing of an Arnold Schwarzenegger double bill to find this e-mail on his screen:

LOVE.
Lords Of Virtual Existence
IRL 3001
S.O.S.
Justine stranded in 1967
Your help needed ASAP
Contact
http://www.love@3001ad.com

Naturally, he responded as you can well imagine:

http://www.love@3001ad.com
HA HA v. funny
GAL

Another message came back almost immediately:

HHOS
Stop being a PITA
and
Bloody well believe it!

At that point Chuck decided to humour whoever it was.

http://www.love@3001ad.com
OK, so I'm a:-) Guy
What can I do for you?

A message came back immediately:

Go to 67 Pratts Lane NOW!

It would be Pratts Lane wouldn't it. Of course, the very address was enough to confirm Chuck in the view that this was just another stupid Net joke.

FOAD
Do you realise what time it is?

Los must have gone berserk at that moment. He started 'flaming' him with every known term of computer abuse. But Chuck just put up the message:

AFK
TTFN

So, he was none too pleased in the morning when he discovered that Los had vented his rage on his father's fax machine. He used up the entire fax roll telling Chuck precisely what he thought of him.

It was Casper, Chuck's father, who was actually on the receiving end of all this electronic abuse. He arrived in Chuck's bedroom with an armful of fax paper which was informing him in vivid language what a brain-dead neanderthal arse-hole he was.

'I assume this is for you, and it isn't Prof. Mansell's response to my article for *Science Today*,' he said. 'At least, I sincerely hope not.'

At that point Maggie, Chuck's mother, received a telephone call from Caroline. Chuck only heard the Maggie end of the conversation.

Maggie: 'No she's not been here.'

The telephone: '........................!!!!'

Maggie: 'Umm. Oh dear. Ummm. Really? . . . I see . . . Oh dear. Yes! . . . No, not friends of his. No . . . Umm . . . Yes . . . I'll ask him.'

The conversation that followed had gone something like this:

Maggie: 'Have you any idea where Justine is?'

Chuck: 'Yep, she's gone off with a load of time travellers and is currently in 1967.'

'Stop fooling around, this is serious.'

'It certainly is. You'd better sort this whole thing out – and fast!' agreed Casper who was putting on his coat in a huff because he had to go out to buy a new roll of fax paper.

So Chuck got back to his keyboard:

http://www.love@3001ad.com
Precisely what have I done to you man?

And the answer came back:

67 Pratts Lane
Plug in the f-ing hardware man
and all will be revealed
;-)

So basically, there was nothing else for it. Chuck simply had to get over there and get it sorted.

After practically shaking the front door off its hinges

knocking and ringing, he'd had one hell of a job breaking in. Being a male it didn't even occur to him to pop round to the back and see if the backdoor was unlocked. But anyway, he'd crept around inside the house giving himself the scare of a lifetime expecting to find me bound and gagged in a cupboard or something. But all he'd found was a computer which was unplugged.

And being Chuck, naturally, he'd plugged it in.

At which point there was the most almighty explosion. Just as I thought there would be. I was right you see!

And I was downloaded in the very same spot as I was uploaded.

'Geesus,' said Chuck, staring at me as if I were a ghost or something. 'Where did you spring from?'

I was standing in a sort of daze, as you can well imagine.

'What are you doing here?' I asked.

'What am *I* doing here? For Chrystsake, Justine. I got this weird e-mail in the middle of the night. I've been flamed with electronic abuse. Flooded with fax paper. Accused by your mother of pimping, procuring, bondage and God knows what else. What else? Oh yes. I've spent the last few hours convinced that I'd find you bound and gagged and held as a sex-slave or something.'

'I wish.'

'Are you OK?'

'No. Yes. I don't know.'

'So what have you been up to? Where are all these weird friends of yours, anyway?'

'I'm not awfully sure . . .'

'You're not about to blub or anything are you?' Chuck had that kind of 'males-can't-cope-with-emotion' look on his face. He groped for his handkerchief.

'Oh Chuck . . .'

He put his arms round me in a big warm hug.

'Come on, baby . . .'

'You're my bestest, bestest friend, you know that don't you?' I sniffed into his anorak.

'Yeah . . . sure . . . unfortunately.'

'I can't think of any way I can ever pay you back.'

'A long, heavy, totally abandoned, sex session might do the trick.'

'Don't be silly.'

'I didn't know I was.'

'Oh Chuck.'

'Here, have a good blow.' He handed me a crumpled hanky.

I did.

'Better? Let's get you home then.'

When we got home Chuck went into the kitchen and closed the door and talked to Caroline for some time. I don't know what he said but whatever it was did the trick. She didn't shout or rant, she just suggested I had a long hot bath. Then I went to bed and slept all through the day and the evening and the night and into the following morning.

And I had the strangest dream. I dreamt my mother had just come into my bedroom dressed in a pink vinyl mini skirt wearing massive false eye-lashes and with her hair all Vidal-Sassooned and was apologising tearfully for the way she had treated me.

'. . . and that really means no curfews ever again?'

'No darling.'

'And you'll never come barging into my room at some unearthly hour and putting the light on?'

'Never.'

'. . . or ask me whether or not I've done my homework?'

'Wouldn't dream of it.'

When I came down for some breakfast, she was standing there wearing her perfectly ordinary Jaeger jumper and mid-calf skirt, thank God. She was still trying to look disapproving, but I noticed she'd put all my favourite breakfast things on the worktop and she'd cut half an orange into segments like a grapefruit for me, the way she used to do when I was a kid. There were definite signs that things weren't going to be too bad.

She made herself a cup of coffee and sat down while I ate.

No, actually, she *didn't* say, 'Would it help to talk about it' – even Caroline's more subtle than that.

She said, 'So what's happened to your Silver Surfer?'

'He's gone.'

'You really liked him, didn't you?'

I nodded.

'These things never last, you know.'

'What about you and Daddy?'

'Oh, we had our ups and downs. We broke up once, you know. There was the most terrible scene. After my sister Hannah's twenty-first . . . . What a night that was . . .'

'Really?' I swallowed a mouthful of orange whole.

'Daddy and I were banned from seeing each other – for ages.'

'Why . . . ?'

'Umm well. Umm, gosh I don't know quite why really. But Grampy had always disapproved of Daddy, even before umm . . .'

(Before you got caught in the shrubbery? I was tempted to prompt her. But thought better of it).

'And I remember now, it's all coming back to me. It was

mainly the fault of this dreadful au pair girl . . . What was her name . . . Heidi? . . . No Helga . . . That was it. She and poor Hannah ran off with this band. The whole thing was simply frightful . . . Do you want some more tea?'

'So what did Helga do that was so terrible?'

But Mummy clammed up at that point and started fussing about having run out of Earl Grey. Typical! Parents!

Then she went into some total non-sequitur about how she had discovered a vastly expensive chap in Harley Street who could actually remove tattoos if paid enough. It seemed she was obviously drawing comfort from the fact that she thought she would be able to persuade me to go and see him.

So I humoured her for a while.

'Oh and by the way,' she ended, 'there's a strange message on that computer thing for you.'

'An e-mail?'

'Don't get technical with me, Justine. It's from America.'

America? Who did I know in America?

I went to the screen.

From: Los Angeles

It was another verse from 'Silver Surfer'. You know, his lyrics. It went:

Venus shine for me
Like the light
From a distant star
Your love
Is in the waves
And the waves from your time
Flow forever into mine
:-x

It was just so, so beautiful.

I sat there for ages looking at it.

I couldn't actually bring myself to use the computer while it was there. So I just sat down in front of the screen at Daddy's desk. That's when something on top of the desk caught my eye. It was the *Daily Telegraph* from my Millennium Project. Right on the front page was the shot of the man with the death's head mask and the 'MAKE LOVE NOT WAR' placard.

And just behind him, unmistakable in Caroline's silver lurex sheath dress, was ME.

I knew I'd seen that guy in the mask somewhere before. Suddenly it all came back to me. How the photographer had taken the picture at precisely that moment. I studied the photo more carefully, it was me all right – I looked such a freak!

This was just what I needed. Proof! At last!

I got on to Chuck right away.

'Look you've got to come over right now. I've got something to show you!'

Chuck arrived within the hour.

He looked quite good actually. He wasn't wearing his dreaded anorak for once. And the funny thing was – Chuck has always had this real 'dweeb' style in the way he dressed and everything. And all of a sudden, as if fate was on his side or something, his 'dweeb' style was the current 'in' look. Incredible but true! He looked really good.

'How are you feeling?' he asked.

Then he caught sight of the computer screen.

'What on earth is that?'

'He sent me an e-mail.'

'What you going to do, put a ribbon round the computer and keep it under your pillow?'

'Just read it,' I said.

He leant over the screen.

'Got a quaint little metaphysical ring to it, I guess,' said Chuck dismissively. Then he stretched out on Daddy's leather couch. 'So are you going to tell me what really happened?'

'I told you. I spent three whole days in 1967.'

'Bollocks.'

'Well, if you're going to be like that.'

'You spent three whole days in 67 Pratt's Lane, making-it with your dick-head on air-waves.'

'God – you're as bad as my parents. That is just not true. Nothing happened, actually.'

'It didn't?' Those little smile lines round his mouth were registering male satisfaction. 'Why not?'

'It just didn't.'

'But you really fancied the boxers off him. Didn't you?'

'No need to be so crude.'

'A bit one-sided was it?'

'Not exactly. We were too different that's all.'

'How.'

'He *is* from the year, 3001.'

'Bullshit!'

'I travelled back in time, didn't I? He just came from a bit further off, that's all.'

'Oh sure.'

'You don't believe me, do you?'

'Nope.'

'What if I had proof?'

He snorted with laughter: 'Such as?'

Chuck settled down more comfortably on the couch, preparing to be sceptical.

I sat holding the *Daily Telegraph* with an expression of modestly concealed triumph.

'Look!' I said, shoving the newspaper under his nose. 'See the date on the paper, *29 July 1967*. And the picture . . . ?'

'Geesus,' said Chuck, sitting up. 'Bloody hell. Chryst. That's you.'

'How's that for proof?'

'Guess you could have had it morphed in . . .' said Chuck examining the photo close up.

'Oh, come off it. Why? For heaven's sake?'

'Well, s'pose it is pretty convincing, in its way . . .' he said grudgingly. 'Yeah. S'pose it is. I mean really. It really is actually.' He took his glasses off and held the newspaper up to the light. 'Really!'

'Convinced now?'

'OMG,' said Chuck. 'You know what this means, don't you?'

I shook my head.

'I've got the whole of that A level project work I've been doing on Stephen Hawking's new revised theory, of his original theory on Einstein's General Theory of Relativity – wrong.'

'I think you lost me a theory or two back.'

'But this is serious, man.'

'I should say it is. I was nearly stranded in 1967.'

'I just can't think where I went wrong.'

'I might *never* have got back.'

'Yes, that really *is* serious,' said Chuck. 'You wouldn't have been marooned there, forever, of course. You'd just have got older and older and would still be around. Only you'd be . . . *forty-six* now.'

'Ghastly!'

'Hideous!' he said. 'You'd be old enough to be my mother! What if I hadn't been around. What if Los hadn't found you. What if . . .' Chuck was deep in thought.

'Hey that's really odd, you know,' he said.

'What?'

'How did he know where to find you?'

I shrugged. 'He was really mysterious about that. He kept on coming out with this code. CP or something with a number after it. They all seemed to think that was terribly funny.'

'CP,' said Chuck. 'Not a standard TLA. Can't think of anything that stands for. CP, CP, CP, unless it's See P., of course. As in See Page.'

'See what page?'

'Some page of some book or something. I mean, that's the thing about the Net. In the long term everything that's ever been in print is going to be in it. Every plan, every map, every blueprint, every film, every photo, every book that's ever been written. It'll all be data in cyberspace . . .'

'Some page in some book?' I interrupted. 'That doesn't help at all. There isn't a book that could tell Los where I was in 1967, is there?'

That's when Chuck stared at me with this strange kind of 'Eureka' look in his eyes. His whole face seemed to say: I've got it. Everything has suddenly come clear!

'There isn't *yet!*' he said.

'What do you mean, *yet*?'

'Because it hasn't been written – *yet*.'

'It hasn't?'

'But it will be. It must be. Or you'd be stuck there forever. And there's only one person who can write it, Justine. There's only one person who knows precisely what happened. Precisely where you were in 1967. Isn't there?'

With a sort of sinking in the stomach, I knew what was coming next.

'Me?'

Chuck nodded.

When Chuck left, I very quietly closed the study door. I sat down in front of the screen and typed the title:

LOVE. in Cyberia

YOUR GUIDE TO CYBERSPEAK

(Supplied by Chuck Neville Davies – FOC)

ACRONYMS:

AFK	Away From Keyboard
B4	Before
BAK	Back At Keyboard
BCNU	Be Seeing You
BTDT	Been There Done That
BTW	By The Way
CP	See Page
EYHO	Eat Your Heart Out
F2F	Face To Face
FAQ	Frequently Asked Questions
FOAD	F*** Off And Die
FOAF	Friend Of A Friend
FOC	Free Of Charge
GAL	Get A Life
HHOJ	Ha Ha Only Joking
HHOS	Ha Ha Only Serious
HOAM	Hang On A Minute
IRL	In Real Life
ITRW	In The Real World

JAM — Just A Minute
KISS — Keep It Simple Stupid
L8R — Later
LTNS — Long Time No See
MORF — Male OR Female?
NFA — No Fixed Abode
NFWM — No F****** Way Man!
OAO — Over and Out
OMG — Oh My God!
OTT — Over The Top
PITA — Pain In The Arse
RUOK — Are You OK?
SITD — Still In The Dark?
TLA — Three Letter Acronym
TNX — Thanks
TTFN — Ta Ta For Now
VR — Virtual Reality
WYSIWYG — What You See Is What You Get

SMILEY CYBERMEN

(Lean head on one side to read. Or turn the book round, dumbo!)

Smiley	Meaning
:-II	Angry
:-)	Happy
:-(	Sad
)	Cheshire cat
:’-(	Crying
:-)’	Drooling
:’’’(	Floods of tears

8)	Frog
::-)	Wearing glasses
:-X	Kiss
(-:	Left-handed
:-I	Monkey
*-)	Stoned
:-))	Very happy
:-((	Very sad
;-)	Winking

CYBERJARGON

Bit	A unit of measurement representing the smallest unit of storage in a computer.
Bits per second	bps the speed at which bits are transmitted.
Byte	A group of binary digits that are stored and operated on as a unit.
Connect Time	The length of time you spend On-line on the Internet.
Crash	A sudden and total system failure.
Cross Post	To post the same message to more than one conference message area.
Cyberbusker	A musician who plays open concerts on the Internet.
Cyberpunk	A person who 'lives' in the future culture of Cyberspace: Like that 'dick-head' Los.
Cyberspace	The 'world' that exists within computer networks.

Download	The transfer of data from another remote computer.
E-mail	Electronic mail. A method of sending messages via computer instead of putting ink on dead trees.
Flame	An abusive or personal attack against the sender of a message.
Gateway	A computer system to transfer data between incompatible networks.
Internet	The worldwide network of computer networks.
Kit	Computer equipment.
Lurker	An individual who looks in on Net newsgroups but doesn't post messages.
Modem	MOdulator/DEModulator a device which converts information you place on your computer into a signal that can be transmitted via the telephone lines to a remote computer and vice-versa.
Net	Commonly used name for the Internet.
Netiquette	The supposed etiquette of the Net.
Newbie	Someone who is new to the Net.
Net Virgin	Someone who has never surfed.
NFA	Individuals of No Fixed Abode – used as Cyberian 'Sleepers' in time. Brilliant highly-motivated cyber-engineers often mistakenly identified as tramps.
Password	A security string of letters or numbers required to be input before access to a system is granted.
Shouting	Sending e-mail messages all in caps.
Smiley	A smiling face character made from

	joining units of punctuation together. Used to express emotions etc.
Snail Mail	The sending of mail by traditional land-based methods i.e. the Post Office.
Spamming	Indiscriminate spreading of irrelevant information across the Internet which basically clogs up e-mail.
Surfer	Someone who surfs cyberspace looking for interesting sites and people to visit.
TCP	Transmission Control Protocol – nothing whatsoever to do with acne control.
TLA	Three Letter Acronym – these, in practice, often contain more than three letters but what the hell – who's counting?
Upgrade	To improve/add features to a system.
Upload	The sending of data from your computer to another remote computer – but used more freely by some nerds, geeks, poseurs, brain-dead neanderthals, I could mention.
Virtual Reality	A computer technology that creates a very real illusion of being in a 3D artificial world. Ask Justine! See *Virtual Sexual Reality*.
Virus	A program designed to infect and sometimes destroy other programs. The cyberlout's version of tearing down trees in the street, or destroying wildlife.

Wibble	Nonsense that turns up in a message area.
World Wide Web	A hypertext information and resource system for the Internet.
WWW	TLA for the above.

Hey man, I left one out!

Connecting	Or 'currently connecting' as Cyberpunks call it. Cyber-slang for what we call 'going out together' – which happens to be what Justine and I are currently doing. She didn't want to let on, but I reckoned we owed it to you to let you know what really happened in the end. EYHO LA CND